QUILT
of
GRACE

Joyce Williams

ABOUT THE AUTHOR

Joyce Williams lives in the beautiful Wenatchee Valley in Eastern Washington. Married for over forty years to husband Paul, she loves history and enjoys traveling, but writing is her passion, along with her family and church. Her first book, *The Lady Rose*, was published by Heartsong. Find her inspirational blog at: *http://www.joycewilliamswritenow.blogspot.com/*

ISBN-10: 1493664964
ISBN-13: 978-1493664962

RECOGNITION

My sincere gratitude and appreciation for the expert skill of Devorah Nelson, "The Story Doctor," *(www.storydoctor.blogspot.com)* who showed me how to make a good story better!

DEDICATION

To all the pioneers who came west by wagon
train, and especially to those who recorded
their adventures in letters and journals:
Thank You!

PROLOGUE

April 11, 1862.

The crocuses bloomed. The tulips. The hyacinths and jonquils. And a cloudless blue sky canopied Austin and Eleanor Cartwright's manicured back lawn, where white wooden collapsible chairs occupied by well-wishing family and friends bordered the flagstone path. Defined by a face-splitting grin, twenty-two-year-old Philip Denbeigh waited in the shade of the ivy-covered pergola for his eighteen-year-old bride, the lovely Lillian Cartwright.

When the starry-eyed young woman dressed in white floated blithely along the rose petal strewn aisle, the two sets of parents struggled to keep their chins steady, their tears in check.

But not for joy.

You see, they knew there would be no happy Sunday family dinners. No prattling babies bouncing on jolly grandparents' old knees. And no tender farewells when eternity beckoned.

Phillip and Lillian felt called to bring civilization and the gospel to the "wild" west. And that meant saying good-bye forever to family and friends.

Their train will be leaving for Independence, Missouri, in three days.

Joyce Williams

CHAPTER ONE

"Jack Montgomery, at your service, Miss." The broad-shouldered young man snatched off his wide-brimmed leather hat with a sun-browned hand, exposing a thatch of mahogany curls. His Southern drawl betrayed his roots. "Forgive my haste," he apologized to the pretty young woman he'd nearly knocked over when he dashed around the end of the covered wagon.

Lillian staggered, regained her balance, and looked up into the handsome stranger's tanned face. Dropping her freshly tied bonnet ribbons, she quickly held out her right hand. "Lillian Denbeigh, Mr. Montgomery. I'm pleased to make your acquaintance." She flashed an open smile at the big man who appeared to be in his late twenties. Friendliness characterized everyone she'd met from Mr. Scranton's wagon train, and Jack Montgomery proved no exception.

"Miss Lily Ann." Employing his best Southern manners, Jack bent to kiss her gloved hand, held firmly in his grip. He lifted his head and met her gaze square on. "That's a pretty name." His brown eyes told her more was pretty than just her name—or was it just his eyes adjusting to the shade cast by the wagon's canvas bonnet?

Suspicious that he was attempting to flirt with her,

Lillian protested in her clipped New England accent, "My name is *not* Lily Ann—it's Lillian. Lillian Denbeigh." Her flustered correction held all the disapproval of a spinster schoolmarm rapping a student's fingers for his giving a wrong answer.

Jack's lips twitched; he might have been fighting a smile but his face was shadowed and it was hard to tell. "Sawry, Mees. Ah meant no harrum," came his decidedly exaggerated drawl. Now she was sure he was flirting with her; there was absolutely nothing about the way he looked at her that could be deemed sincere.

Lillian snatched back her hand, impulsively peeled off her left glove, and thrust out her hand to display the gleaming gold wedding band circling her third finger. "It's Mrs., not Miss . . . *Mrs.* Denbeigh." She tilted her head as she established a social boundary, "My husband is the Reverend Phillip Denbeigh."

"You're the Reverend's missus?" Shock replaced admiration in Mr. Montgomery's eloquent brown eyes.

"Yes, I am." Lillian cast an almost imperceptible sanctimonious glance down her pointed little nose. "We plan to start a church in Oregon territory." She took her time smoothing her glove over her slender fingers.

"Hmm." Jack raised one bushy eyebrow, shrugged a well-developed shoulder, and gave a short chuckle. "Some folk are heathen by choice."

Her blue eyes flew to his like homing pigeons. "Are you telling me you're one of them?" she blurted out, rattled to her core. If his goal was to shock her, he'd succeeded; in her sheltered world no one blatantly professed to be an unbeliever—that was the condition of wild tribesmen in the far reaches of the world and the uncivilized souls they were going west to evangelize. She clutched at her bonnet ribbons, tugging so hard the bow came untied.

"Am I a heathen?" Jack's brown eyes laughed at her; it was his turn to enjoy her discomfiture. He raked his fingers through his hair, rendering his curls boyishly mussed as he boasted, "Without a doubt." Replacing his stylish "Boss of the Plain" Stetson hat at a jaunty angle, he nonchalantly hooked his thumbs in the waistband of his well-fitting breeches, as if to say, So what do you think of that?

Lillian pursed her bow-shaped lips then made him a prim promise, "I'll be praying for you, Mr. Montgomery."

"You do that, Miss Lily Ann. *Your* prayers just might work." His smirk said he was teasing her again.

"Oh, I expect they will, Mr. Montgomery." She methodically retied her bonnet ribbons and moved her mild sarcasm to reproof, "Phillip says God *always* answers our prayers."

As if he'd heard his name, Phillip Denbeigh emerged around the corner of the wagon. His high, furrowed brow beneath his raven-black hair smoothed when he saw his pretty wife. "There you are, my dear. I was worried when I didn't find you at our wagon."

Lillian jumped, startled. She didn't even know why; she wasn't doing anything wrong.

"Good day, Miss Lily Ann. Reverend Denbeigh."

Jack suppressed a smile, politely raised his hat, and sauntered away, disappearing around the end of the wagon.

Lillian spoke quickly to forestall the questions brimming in her young husband's intense blue eyes. "Mr. Montgomery was just introducing himself. When he learned that I am the *Reverend* Denbeigh's wife, he informed me that he is a heathen—by choice!"

Phillip's wide mouth tipped in his endearingly crooked smile. "Well, it's reassuring to know our services are needed, perhaps sooner than we anticipated."

Catching a whiff of her husband's sage soap as he straightened his clerical collar, Lillian relaxed and returned his grin. Her small hand slipped through the crook in his arm, and she affectionately rested her bonneted head against his shoulder.

"We'll just have to include him in our prayers," Phillip concluded.

Lillian nodded. Prayer was Phillip's solution to everything. And she had determined to be his apt pupil. "That's what I told him. But he seemed to think it was a joke."

"Well, we'll pray that God will help him see his need," Phillip patted her gloved hand where it rested on his sleeve, "which puts me in mind of something else." His assessing gaze swept over the men milling about in the common area inside the wagon circle, their loud voices intruding on his comments. "Not all men are gentlemen, Lill, so please, do be careful when I'm not with you." As her fingers tightened on his arm he quickly downplayed the danger, "Just a word of caution." He pressed a reassuring kiss on her upturned mouth.

"Roll call. Roll call." Mr. Scranton's booming voice was followed by a long trumpet blast.

Phillip clasped Lillian's hand and tugged. "Come, we don't want to be late." Eager to get acquainted with the members of their traveling party, the newlyweds hurried toward the gathering on the open grass inside the wagon circle.

As far as one could see, wagons and tents covered the landscape surrounding Independence, and more travelers arrived each day. Children ran and shouted, jumping over wagon tongues and tripping over tent pegs. Babies cried and dogs barked and growled. The cattle lowed and bawled and sometimes bellowed, and when a breeze came up, pungent barnyard smells tainted the air. Lillian had never heard so much noise or seen so much commotion in her whole sheltered life, and she had to admit it made her nervous; she was anxious to get in their wagon and start rolling toward Oregon.

An hour later, instructions and introductions completed, Phillip and Lillian headed hand-in-hand toward their wagon to await their turn—they were number thirty-five of sixty-two—as the wagons lined up in the order of the lots drawn. Lillian was pleased to learn that each morning the front wagon dropped back to last position so everyone had a turn breathing clean air at the front of the train.

She climbed into the wagon and perched on the large Shaker hope chest, a present from her parents for her sixteenth birthday. She grabbed up the double wedding ring pattern quilt crafted by her mother's missionary society friends at her church back home and spread it out, studying for the hundredth time the words embroidered in each of the nine interlocking rings: **HOPE, PATIENCE, COURAGE, PEACE, TRUST, REST, COMFORT, LOVE, GRACE.** The quilt was her most cherished possession, presented to her at a bridal tea held in her honor.

Lillian closed her eyes and pictured the long buffet table in the church fellowship hall. A finely-woven linen tablecloth trimmed in Alencon lace provided the backdrop for a collection of tasty tea items. Three-tiered trays featured dainty triangle-shaped crustless sandwiches spread with butter and filled with minced ham and thin cucumber slices. Footed crystal bowls brimmed with fruit relish, beet pickles, and sweet baby gherkins. Silver platters displayed mincemeat pastries, rich almond tea cakes, and light-as-a-feather scones with accompanying lemon curd, raspberry jam, and clotted cream. And best of all, a plate of her favorite lemon tarts. She licked her lips, tasting again in her imagination the flavorful lemon custard.

And oh, what she wouldn't give for a glass of cold lemonade poured from her fondly-remembered Grandmother Cartwright's ice-frosted pitcher and sipped out of one of a dozen matching fluted crystal goblets. The set had been a wedding gift she'd brought along on the train in a trunk and then repacked into a keg of cornmeal to prevent breakage on the wagon journey. And her mother's flower-sprigged china plates that made every bite taste like ambrosia, also a gift, had been carefully layered between the linens in her hope chest.

She let her mind dwell on the conclusion to the bridal tea. Her mother's missionary society friends had presented her with this special "encouragement quilt," suggesting it should be a constant reminder of their commitment to pray for her every day.

The wagon shook as Phillip, having seen to the oxen, climbed up and over the spring seat. Lillian put out her hand to steady herself and looked up as Phillip ducked his head to avoid a branch of the lilac bush her mother had insisted on sending with them, along with the reminder that it was a start from the original bush brought with her English ancestors when they came to America.

Settling on the crate of hymnals, Phillip hunched forward. "Let's pray before we get going." He grabbed Lillian's hand.

As they bowed their heads, he prayed fervently, "Dear Heavenly Father, thank You for this opportunity to do Your work. Please give us a safe journey, and help us encourage the many believers who are seeking to follow You as they pursue a better life for their families. Give Mr. Scranton wisdom as he leads us. And finally, we mention Mr. Montgomery, who has by his own mouth exposed his need for You. Use us as your instruments to bring him to repentance and salvation. We are grateful for Your goodness to us. We ask these things in the name of Your blessed Son, Jesus. Amen."

Echoing Phillip's amen, Lillian smoothed her free hand over the bottom right segment of the quilt facing up on her lap. With her index finger she traced the word **HOPE** embroidered in purple floss on a white background and surrounded by a fabric circle of purple iris blooms. Hope certainly seemed like the right word to describe how she felt.

* * *

Phillip poked his head into the wagon. "Stay here, Lill. I'm going ahead to see what's causing the delay." The wagon shook as he jumped to the ground.

Lillian climbed out between the front flaps and settled on the spring seat. She watched Phillip skirt their two pairs of yoked oxen, admiring his compact physique as he approached the Harmon wagon in front of them.

The sky was clear and seemed much bluer than the often foggy coastal New England sky she'd known her whole life; she couldn't help thinking it reminded her of the luminous underside of the domed lid of her mother's Blue Onion soup tureen, and she felt certain she'd never get tired of looking up.

When Lewis Harmon joined Phillip, the two men moved forward and soon disappeared.

Lillian retrieved her dainty white handkerchief—one of the imported linen ones from her trousseau, embroidered with an embellished "*D*" for Denbeigh and smelling of lavender—from its discreet hiding place under her starched white cuff. She patted her forehead, nose, chin, neck. Mid-morning of their first day and already she was miserably warm; this sultry Missouri weather made her miss the cool ocean breezes of home.

"'ello."

Lillian lowered her handkerchief.

A little boy's tousled blonde head poked out from the back of the Harmon wagon. His dimpled chin rested on the backboard and his two round blue eyes, brimming with curiosity, stared at her over the backs of the oxen.

Glad for the diversion, she called out, "Hello yourself. My name is Lillian. What's yours?"

The cherubic face immediately vanished behind the canvas curtain, reminding Lillian of a puppet bobbing off stage in a children's puppet show. She chuckled as she slipped her handkerchief back inside her cuff.

Suddenly, *two* strawberry blonde heads popped into the opening between the flaps, their sweet little faces as alike as two peas. "Mama says we can talk to you," the boy announced, flashing a full set of tiny white baby teeth.

"Oh, that's nice." Lillian smiled and said again, "My name is Lillian Denbeigh. What's yours?"

The girl's dimpled, rosy cheeks, framed by flaxen curls, plumped in a grin that displayed another perfect set of pearly baby teeth. "I'm Emily. I'm five. And this here is Evan. He's three." She smacked the top of her brother's head with more force than finesse. "We have a sister, too, but she's a baby and can't do anything yet."

"Uh, 'cept eat and cry and wet." Evan stated the obvious.

Don't you dare laugh, Lillian, she admonished herself, disciplining her snicker.

"All babies do that, Dummy," Emily scoffed, the blatantly confident big sister.

"Well, I don't remember being a baby, so I wouldn't know." Evan slid his hands behind his dark blue overall bib as if to shield himself from his big sister's bossiness.

Quick to prevent a quarrel, Lillian interrupted, "What's your baby sister's name?"

"Elizabeth," Emily answered promptly. An enthusiastic bounce toppled her from her perch and forced her to give attention to righting herself.

"Elizabeth *Anne*." Evan took advantage of his big sister's distraction, his face beaming at having the last word.

Emily and Evan were two of the most adorable children Lillian had ever seen. Oh, she did want children of her own. *Please, God, give me a baby,* she sent her silent prayer heavenward. An only child, Lillian envied friends blessed with brothers and sisters, and she'd concluded the only way she'd ever enjoy that sense of family was to have her own children. She felt fortunate that Phillip, the oldest of seven siblings, shared her enthusiasm for children. In fact, Phillip's affectionate interaction with his younger brothers and sisters was what had first attracted her to him.

Each summer, Phillip's family visited his grandparents and his aunts, uncles, and cousins who lived in her same town. She'd watched them laugh and joke in the churchyard following Sunday services and noted that Phillip always watched out for the safety of the younger ones.

When Phillip came to stay with his relatives during the Christmas holiday a year ago, his cousins brought him to the church's annual holiday box social. Topped with a sprig of fresh holly and tied with a bright red ribbon fashioned into a soft bow, Lillian's wicker basket caught Phillip's eye—and despite fierce competition, he resolutely won the bid. To her smug delight, he confessed later that he'd seen her deliver her basket through the back door of the church earlier in the day, so his determination was based on more than just a bit of holly and a bright bow.

Smiling at her memory of their first evening spent together getting acquainted, Lillian's thoughts returned to reality when her reverie was interrupted by a young woman who poked her head out of the wagon and smiled at her above the children's heads.

A white ruffled apron topped her blue and white gingham check dress that matched her forget-me-not blue eyes, and her friendly greeting made it easy to see why her children felt at ease with strangers.

"Hi, I'm Betsey Harmon," she dropped her gaze to her infant in arms, "and this is the baby that can't do anything—yet." Lillian joined in Betsey's bubbling laughter.

"How do you do? I'm Lillian Denbeigh." She nodded at the baby. "How old is she?" The baby hiccupped and then gurgled. Her face wrinkled around a gummy grin and her arms and legs pumped with infant joy.

"Four months next week," Betsey replied, smoothing her hand over Elizabeth's downy head and ending at her chin, where she wiped away the drool. "Just right for traveling: young enough to stay put but not so young as to easily take sick. If she's anything like the other two, I won't have to worry about her getting into things until we're settled somewhere."

Eager to get better acquainted, Lillian leaned forward. "Where are you from?"

"Warrensburg, Missouri." Betsey tucked a flyaway strand of blonde hair behind her left ear and added, "I was content there, but Lewis said it was getting too crowded. He likes open spaces because he loves to hunt."

Emily piped up, obviously parroting an overheard adult conversation, "The settlers have killed all the wild game. That's why we're moving west."

Betsey nodded and bestowed an indulgent smile on her cherub-cheeked daughter. "I'm not rightly fond of guns myself, but I surely do appreciate the meat he brings home." Her gaze shifted to Lillian. "Does your husband relish hunting?"

Lillian wrinkled her forehead, a vague expression clouding her eyes. "Ah, I don't really know. Phillip just graduated from seminary, and we plan to start a church in Oregon." She added an afterthought, "He did buy a gun, though." She smiled, certain she'd preserved her husband's manliness in her new friend's eyes.

But Betsey's attention had caught on Lillian's earlier statement. Her face glowed as she exclaimed, "A church? How wonderful." Her relieved sigh was audible. "I've been worried about what we'd do for . . . well, our church was such an important part of our lives. We helped each other in so many ways—like a big family. My mother died when I was eight, so several older ladies in our church taught me how to cook and clean and care for my children." She looked around, noting that Emily and Evan had ducked back into the wagon.

"I brought along a tin box filled with recipes." Lillian hesitated before admitting a bit self-consciously, "My family always had a cook so my skills are pretty simple."

"Maybe we could read through the recipes together. I'm always looking for new ideas." Betsey's tactful warmth solidified their friendship.

"The tin is stored in our big trunk," Lillian made a wry face, "but the lid is too heavy to lift by myself. I'll ask Phillip to get it for me the next time he opens the trunk." A rivulet of perspiration trickled down her cheek, and she retrieved her handkerchief from her cuff and patted it away.

"What supplies did you bring along?" Betsey changed the subject.

Holding up her gloved fingers, Lillian concentrated on ticking off the items recommended by Mr. Tyler at the mercantile in Independence. "Two hundred pounds each of flour, cornmeal, and smoked bacon; thirty pounds of dried jerky; twenty pounds each of coffee, salt, molasses, and white sugar; five pounds of brown sugar; a tub of lard; ten jars of currant jelly; a hundred pounds each of dried beans and rice; a keg of vinegar; three blocks of cheese; ten pounds of dried yeast; sourdough starter, a big box of soap flakes; and a crock of baking soda. My mother sent garden seeds and a lilac bush."

Her face brightened, "Oh, and we have two crates filled with Bibles and hymnals. For starting a church, you know. When the Session in my church back home learned of our plan to start a church in Oregon, they bought new ones and gave us all the old ones." She chuckled, "*St. Matthew's Presbyterian* is printed on them, so I guess our church already has a name."

Betsey's eyes lit up. "We're Presbyterians, too. And so are the Lawsons, the Coopers, the Hoyles, and the Newcombs. We were all part of the Warrensburg Oregon Society."

"What is the Warrens—pardon me, what did you call it?"

"Warrensburg Oregon Society," Betsey repeated,

bending down to retrieve the handmade yarn doll that Elizabeth had dropped. "We got together once a month to read traders' and trappers' journals, government reports, missionaries' stories, and letters from new settlers. We've been planning and saving for four years to make this trip. Most of us women have some fears, but our husbands are quite deter—"

"Do either of you know why we're stopped?" Both women turned to see who owned the sultry, thickly-accented contralto that interrupted their conversation.

"I'm Desiree Vargas," the black-haired young woman identified herself, "with the Velasquez party." She jerked her curly head toward the wagons lined up behind the Denbeigh wagon. "We're four wagons back. Maria Velasquez is my cousin."

She shifted her weight onto one leg and extended the other out from her torso in a pose that emphasized her long legs, small waist, and full bosom threatening to overflow her low-cut square-necked white blouse. A musky scent emanated from her—strong enough to make Lillian sneeze. Twice.

Betsey rescued the awkward situation. "I'm Mrs. Lewis Harmon. How do you do, Miss Vargas?"

"And I'm Reverend Denbeigh's wife." Lillian suddenly felt cold; she shivered despite the heat. "Our husbands have gone ahead—for that very reason."

"Your men have gone ahead?" Desiree purred, shifting her narrowed gaze and her interest to the wagons in front of them.

Speechless, Betsey and Lillian gaped at her.

Desiree turned back. Eying their shocked faces through sultry black slits, she shook back her long dark hair and abruptly resumed her quest. Her shapely hips swayed provocatively as she disappeared toward the head of the train.

The raised-brow look exchanged by Lillian and Betsey needed no words; they understood each other perfectly. That woman was no lady.

Phillip and Lewis returned a half hour later with a report: A fallen tree had forced the wagons to a halt until the men removed it and cleared the trail.

CHAPTER TWO

The sky flushed a brilliant shade of pink each morning as the sun's first rays broke over the horizon. A sentry's wake-up gunshot got everyone moving, and by seven o'clock the wagons were rolling again. The Scranton-led train had made good time despite the rough trail. Today they'd traveled over eleven miles before noon. Lillian's heart leaped when she overheard Lewis Harmon tell Phillip that at the rate they were traveling, they surely would make it to the Pacific coast in less than the estimated five months.

When the Wakarusa River came into view in the early afternoon, the train slowed to a crawl. The leading wagon approached the narrow, shallow water-way and rolled to a stop. Flanked on both sides by wide, muddy banks, the river was obviously unsafe to cross; all that mud would mire the wagon wheels.

"We're going to build a bridge," Phillip told her upon his return from a hastily-called meeting of the men.

"Build a bridge?" Lillian echoed; she couldn't imagine such a feat taking less than a month—or even two.

"We'll gather up all the wood we can find: poles, small branches, brush, trees. Then we'll lay the longest and thickest logs across the muddy banks and over the water. Next, we'll place smaller branches and poles crosswise on top of them. Mr. Scranton said the bridge will be bumpy to ride across, but it will keep the wagon wheels from sticking in the mud.

"H-How long will it take—to build a bridge?"

"Three, maybe four days. Why?"

She hesitated then said reluctantly, "I really need to do some laundry."

Understanding dawned in Phillip's blue eyes. "Ah, you need water—and there's a whole lot of mud between it and you." He grinned at her, "You're in luck, Mrs. Denbeigh. That's what you have me for!" He grabbed two large buckets from their hooks on the side of the wagon and braved the mud before he joined the men in their search for wood.

While the water heated over her fire, Lillian got out her washtub, soap flakes, and bag of dirty clothes. As she settled in the shade of her wagon, Betsey called to her from between the rear flaps of the Harmon wagon.

"I have a lot more dirty clothes for five of us than you have for just two. Do you think I'll have time to get them all washed and dried?"

"Yes," Lillian nodded and smiled up at her friend, "plenty of time. Phillip said the men are going to build a bridge so we can cross without getting stuck in the mud. He thinks it could take three or four days. Just bring your tubs, clothes, and soap flakes. I'll share my water; I have more than I need."

In Lillian's childhood home, Portia, the housemaid,

took care of their laundry, and it appeared, clean and folded, in their lavender-scented drawers as if by magic. In preparation for the journey west, Portia had demonstrated how to use a scrub board—but Lillian hadn't been prepared for the way her soft hands chafed in the harsh lye soap and her knuckles rubbed against the board until the tender skin split. She had mourned the sad state of her once beautiful hands and finally resorted to designating a pair of cotton gloves for wear during scrubbing.

Within a few minutes, Betsey was settled in the grass beside Lillian. The two women, surrounded by mounds of dirty clothes, soaped and scrubbed while Emily and Evan played nearby and baby Elizabeth slept in the padded box Lewis had made for her.

They had a good view of the wood-gathering and bridge-building, and as the men worked, they watched another wagon train park a short distance up-river. As the day wore on, Lillian nodded toward the newly arrived wagons and voiced her thoughts. "Those wagons will need to cross, too. Maybe they'll offer to help our men build the bridge."

"After meeting some of the people in our train—" Betsey hesitated then added in a confiding whisper, "like that Vargas woman, maybe we're better off if they don't!" They exchanged a knowing look and went on scrubbing.

When every garment had been washed and rinsed, Lillian and Betsey strung lines between their wagons and hung their wet clothes to dry. Petticoats, shirts, breeches, sheets, pillowcases, and necessities swayed and flapped in the breeze, and several times Betsey had to remind her children not to play hide and seek behind them.

The next morning, after Phillip joined the men to work on the bridge, Lillian mixed up a batch of sourdough bread and set the loaves to raise. Her first attempts at baking bread in her Dutch oven had resulted in loaves that were burned on the bottom, doughy on the top, and full of air pockets; she couldn't figure out how to cook the tops of her loaves without overcooking the bottoms, and her inexperienced kneading lacked the force necessary to produce a smooth, even-grained texture. However, after several frustrating failures, Betsey suggested that hot coals heaped on the lid of her Dutch oven would provide all-around heat and placing a flat rock in the pan first would distribute the bottom heat more evenly. Now she felt proud of her determined efforts—her last two batches had baked evenly with no air bubbles.

Taking advantage of the wagon's stationary status, Lillian swept the exposed floor space with her straw broom before she prepared the noon meal. In the afternoon she collected the dried clothes from the clothesline and dampened and rolled those needing to be pressed—just the way Portia had demonstrated.

While the bread was baking, she cut a thick slice from a flitch of smoked bacon, chopped it into bite-sized pieces, and added it to her pot of pre-soaked beans. When the bread was baked, she put the beans and bacon over the fire to boil into a hearty soup so the evening meal would be ready when Phillip returned.

Later that evening after the dishes were washed and put away, the Dutch oven oiled, and the left-over food safely stored in the wagon, Phillip invited his wife to go for a walk, to view the men's handiwork on the bridge.

When they turned to retrace their steps, Lillian nodded toward the train of wagons still parked up-river. "Won't they need to cross, too? Have any of their men come over to help with the bridge?"

Phillip lowered his voice. "No one has stirred outside their camp since they arrived. Some of our men wanted to talk to them but Mr. Scranton forbade them; he thinks maybe they have the cholera."

"Cholera?" Lillian frowned and immediately picked up her pace. She'd rarely been sick because her mother had kept her at home when schoolmates at the exclusive girls' academy she'd attended came down with the usual childhood illnesses like measles and chicken pox.

Lillian was only too glad to get back to their wagon. She didn't really know much about the disease, but the serious way Phillip said it made her feel anxious.

After breakfast the next morning, Lillian built up her fire, heated her small iron the way Portia had instructed her, and pressed the clean clothes, only burning her fingers once. In the afternoon, she baked a pan of cornbread and a batch of biscuits, determined to take advantage of the opportunity to prepare food during daylight instead of cooking over an evening fire. The biscuits burned on the bottom because she got distracted watching the men at work, but she carefully cut off the black bottom of each one, consoling herself that Phillip preferred the soft tops anyway.

The men finished the bridge in time for the evening meal but there was no singing or visiting afterwards; everyone went to bed early, anticipating that the crossing would make tomorrow a long day.

When the gun blasted the wake-up call at five o'clock the next morning, an hour earlier than usual, everyone hurried through their preparations. Lillian donned her custom-sewn yellow dotted Swiss dress— part of the trousseau provided by her parents. She combed her hair and tied her bonnet ribbons under her chin.

When their tent and bedding were stowed in the wagon, she quickly prepared coffee, bacon, and cornbread for their breakfast while Phillip hitched up the oxen and maneuvered them into place. They were now sixth in line; today it was Jack Montgomery's turn to lead the wagons.

As she stored the last of the breakfast things, Lillian heard someone call out, "Cholera, my foot!"

She leaned over her quilt-draped hope chest and poked her head out the front of the wagon. A sudden chill washed over her body. The other wagon train, the one parked up-river, was driving straight for their newly finished bridge.

With a shout, Jack raced for his wagon.

"Make haste! Let's go!" The cry went up from one wagon to the next.

Phillip jumped up on the spring seat and cracked his whip over their oxen, yelling, "Gee! Gee!"

As their wagon lurched forward, Lillian clung to her hope chest with her chin smashed against the word **PATIENCE** embroidered in pink floss and surrounded by a fabric ring of pink impatiens.

Wide-eyed, she watched Mr. Scranton and several other men gallop up and ride their horses alongside Jack's oxen, and in no time those slow, lumbering creatures were thudding toward the bridge as if they sensed the urgency in the noise around them. Churns, water barrels, pots, and tools rattled on the sides of the wagons as everyone fell into line. Men shouted. Boys yelled. Whips snapped and cracked in the air. Dogs barked. And the rumbling of all the wagons—from both parties—reminded Lillian of the roar of steam engines arriving and departing at the train depot in Independence.

Lillian held her breath. If Mr. Montgomery could just get to the bridge first . . .

Excitement flowed from her head to her toes as she abandoned her dignity and shouted shamelessly, "Go! Go! Go!"

Jack's team and the leading wagon from the other train raced for the bridge. They were side by side now, almost there.

Fear spiraled down Lillian's spine. "Oh, God, please help Mr. Montgomery," she mouthed the words but no sound came out of her stricken throat.

In the tension-fraught silence, Jack raised his whip and brought it down hard on the backs of his oxen. The strength went out of Lillian's legs as the clumsy, galumphing beasts bellowed their surprise and surged ahead.

When Jack raised his whip a second time, the other driver tightened his grip on his reins and sheepishly nodded his defeat. As he turned his oxen aside, his wagon plowed into the mud. And Jack, sitting straight and tall on his spring seat, just kept driving his team . . . straight across the bridge.

A shout of triumph filled the air, accompanied by shrill whistles and cracking whips. The remaining wagons followed immediately behind Jack, leaving no gaps.

It took more than a few repairs to the bridge, but the Scranton party's sixty-two wagons and all their livestock crossed safely over the Wakarusa River. Elation at the justice of the day dominated the campfire discussions that evening, and Jack Montgomery was hailed a hero.

CHAPTER THREE

Her teeth chattering in the chilly morning air, Lillian folded her quilt into a triangle and flung it around her shoulders. To shut out the cold, she flapped one end over the other under her chin. The word **COURAGE**, embroidered in brown floss and circled with fabric pieces featuring brown-eyed daisies, covered her heart like a badge. Hugging the quilt to her chest, she leaned forward and peered at the thermometer mounted just inside the front of the wagon—a costly and thoughtful farewell gift from Phillip's parents.

"Thirty-eight degrees!" No point in hiding her dismay. This was the lowest reading since their departure from Independence. The cold wind, blowing intermittently from the northeast, nagged at the edges of their tent and whipped the oilcloth covers on the wagons, causing them to make loud, erratic, smacking noises. Cattle had bawled all night and the little ewes could still be heard crying with cold feet. No wonder her hands felt stiff and her whole body ached. She'd never been so cold in her life.

"The oxen are ready to go, Lill," Phillip interrupted her thoughts, his voice calling to her from outside the wagon. "And I've brought some kindling for the fire."

Suddenly reminded of her responsibility to prepare breakfast, Lillian scrambled onto the spring seat and then hastily jumped to the ground.

Shielded from the weather by his full-length oilskin duster and wide-brimmed leather hat, Phillip materialized beside the wagon like a ghost come to life. As he eyed his wife's shivering figure, his armload of sticks and spindly twigs tumbled into the hollow where their fire had burned last night. He raised her chin with his finger and grinned as he encouraged her, "We'll both feel better with breakfast and hot coffee in our stomachs, now won't we?" He dropped a quick kiss on her lips.

"You're right," she agreed with Phillip's optimism. "There's nothing so bad that breakfast and a cup of hot coffee can't make it better."

Giving her a gentle pat on her back, Phillip suggested thoughtfully, "Go put on your coat; I'll get the fire started."

As Lillian exchanged her quilt for her bonnet and tailored gray wool coat, she admonished herself under her breath: *As God's emissary I can't let something as trivial as a patch of miserable weather get me down. After all, we've traveled nearly a hundred miles without serious trouble, so I really should be grateful.*

Her stomach growled as she beat the batter for pancakes.

"The fire's ready," Phillip called up to her. "I'll be back shortly."

A tin plate, her well-greased cast iron skillet, a flat

metal spatula, the bowl of pancake batter, two tin cups, the coffee kettle . . . balancing the breakfast makings in her hands, Lillian made three trips from the wagon to the ground.

As she fried the pancakes, the wind picked up force. It snaked around her ankles in harsh gusts and whipped her skirt against her legs. She braced herself as she slid the last pancake on the top of the stack on the tin plate. Belatedly, she realized she'd forgotten to make the coffee first. She sighed out loud at the fleeting thought of Nora, their cook back home, who always had coffee brewing before the family got up in the morning.

When she grabbed the wooden handle of her empty coffee kettle and went to fill it with water from the barrel on the side of the wagon, a blast of wind extinguished her struggling blaze. Staring at the smoldering half-burned sticks, Lillian chewed on her lower lip.

When another gust of wind, stronger than the last, sent her staggering, she made an abrupt decision—no coffee. She filled their tin cups with tepid water. Balancing the plate of pancakes and the cups of water, she climbed into the wagon.

On her second trip to get the empty coffee kettle, the batter bowl, and the skillet, a clap of thunder, louder than any she'd ever heard, so startled Lillian that she tumbled into the wagon. She dropped the skillet and the coffee kettle and barely managed to hang onto the batter bowl when she crashed onto the lid of her hope chest. The rumbling went on and on, echoing as if it would never stop. She suppressed a shudder as she righted herself and retrieved the skillet and kettle from the wagon floor.

Rain began to fall, hard, beating against the wagon like cascading marbles. This was nothing like the drizzling mist they called rain back home, she mused as she put away the breakfast items. Then her glance fell on the word **PEACE**; embroidered in yellow floss and ringed by a buttercup print, it stared up at her from her folded quilt resting on the crate of hymnals.

"Thank you, missionary society ladies. Great reminder," Lillian murmured, shivering in spite of her coat. She grabbed up the "encouragement quilt" and draped it around her shoulders. Leaning her elbows on her hope chest, she pushed aside the front wagon flaps and peered through the pounding rain, looking for Phillip.

Shortly, Lillian saw him materialize from the mist. His clenched fist smashed his hat on his head to prevent the wind from snatching it as he dashed to the wagon. Phillip clutched the sideboard with both hands, swung himself up to the spring seat, and then bounded inside, obviously anxious to get out of the wind and rain. His muddy boots and dripping duster trailed a sloppy mess in his wake.

As he settled on the crate of hymnals, he heaved a loud sigh of relief. Ducking his head and hunching over to avoid the lilac bush, he muttered a brief grace before eagerly taking the plate of molasses-drizzled pancakes and the cup of tepid water that Lillian held out to him.

Too cold to talk, they ate their breakfast in shivering silence.

When the Harmon wagon in front of them started to move, Phillip stuffed his last bite of pancake in his mouth and washed it down with a final gulp of water.

"Thanks, Lill," he said, thrusting his plate and cup toward Lillian before he climbed out the front. Settling on the spring seat, he snapped his whip above the oxen and started them moving.

As the wagon lurched forward, Lillian lost her balance. She grabbed for the lilac bush and didn't let go until they were moving at a steady pace. Eyeing the floor boards tracked with mud, her mouth twisted with frustration; where was Portia when she needed her? This weather would require constant vigilance to keep their belongings clean and dry.

The pounding rain sluiced down the outside of the canvas bonnet on both sides of the wagon, and although the beveled sideboards insured that most of the water splashed on the ground, some dribbled inside at several points where the canvas had worked loose. Hastily, Lillian stuffed towels in the gaps to catch the leakage and then spent the morning rotating the towels and squeezing out the water in an effort to keep the double-bagged canvas sacks filled with coffee, beans, and rice that sat on wooden crates near the leaks, free from moisture damage. Although her arms and hands ached and she felt like crying along with the rain, she didn't dare cease her vigil.

Standing water in the ruts and holes in the trail

churned into mud. The train slowed to a crawl as the wagons bounced along, mile after mile, like a rheumatic caterpillar.

Lillian always welcomed the *nooning*, the mid-day stop that provided a respite from the teeth-jarring ride or the endless walking—she did often walk beside the wagon; but not today, not in the rain.

By the time they stopped for lunch, the rain had reduced to a drizzle. While Phillip cared for the oxen, Lillian quickly lifted the lid on her bread box and took a deep breath of the enticing aroma. Wielding her knife, she cut two slices from the round loaf she'd baked over the open fire the night before.

She stared at the crooked slices, grudgingly admitting that nothing her mother had tried to tell her about the practical challenges of living without servants had dimmed her starry-eyed zeal or prepared her for her own ineptness. She shrugged her shoulders and cheerfully reassured herself that by the time she got used to this primitive life, they would be in Oregon.

When she'd folded the bread slices in half around generous slabs of strong cheese and added some left-over cornbread to each plate and drizzled it with molasses, she poked her head out the front of the wagon to look for Phillip.

"Come! Let's eat," she called down as Phillip approached. "I'm so glad it has stopped raining."

"Let's put a blanket on the seat and enjoy the sunshine," he suggested, eyeing the ribbons of sunlight breaking through the clouds. Content to eat in quietness, they breathed in the rain-fresh air and stared out over the grassy plain that stretched for miles until it met up with the horizon.

As Lillian chewed her last bite, a distant, low rumble disturbed their peace. The rumble grew louder. And closer. Then a train of wagons headed back toward Independence rolled into view. Phillip shot to his feet in alarm. "I hope there isn't Indian trouble up ahead," his anxious words expressed their ever-present fear.

The passing wagons threw up mud that sent Phillip and Lillian scrambling back inside their wagon. But the ruts soon grew dry. The wheels spit dirt, filling the air with grit and making each breath a chore—even inside the shelter of their wagon.

When the last wagon lumbered past, Phillip scraped away the mud from the spring seat and then leaped to the ground. He quickly wiped down the jockey box, the kettle, the axe head, the tools, and the water keg before the mud had a chance to dry. As he finished, thunder rumbled in the distance, fast-moving clouds rolled in and blotted out the sun, and then it began to rain again—although not a torrent this time; just a thick, drizzling mist.

Lillian poked her head out the front of the wagon to check on Phillip and was surprised when a mud-splashed chestnut stallion carrying an equally splattered rider emerged from the haze and drew alongside their wagon. A mud-speckled leather hat shaded the rider's eyes and a brown kerchief covered the lower half of his face.

As the newcomer lowered the kerchief, Lillian's curious eyes collided with Jack Montgomery's warm gaze. Heat instantly rose from her chest to her face, sending her ducking back inside the wagon.

She frowned and swallowed hard. She was happily married, so why did she feel so vulnerable? She grabbed up her quilt and hugged it to her chest like a protective shield.

"Mr. Montgomery. Good to see you," she heard Phillip greet the bigger-than-life Southerner. "Your bravery at the Wakarusa was much appreciated."

She peeked around the wagon flap in time to see Jack raise his hat.

"Thank you, Reverend Denbeigh." Jack's smile gleamed white in his tanned face. "I thought you might be interested to know the train that just passed us is headed back to Independence. Their captain drowned in the Kaw River while moving his cattle across. He left behind an ailing wife and four young children."

"Oh, I'm sorry to hear it," compassion filled Phillip's voice. Then he tipped his head slightly and inquired, "How much farther to the Kaw?"

Listening intently, Lillian stayed out of sight, hidden in the shadow of the canvas bonnet.

"Mr. Scranton says we should reach it by noon tomorrow. But we'll have to wait there a couple of days, at the very least. Boulders cover the river bottom and there's no ferry, so it's slow crossing, one wagon at a time. The men in the train that just passed said there were at least three hundred wagons waiting to cross when they left yesterday afternoon."

"Three hundred!" Shock sent Lillian's head poking out from behind the canvas. Her startled eyes flew to Jack's face.

"Yes, Miss Lily Ann." His sardonic grin sent her gaze to his duster-covered chest. "All waiting to cross the Kaw."

"Why so many?" Phillip asked.

"It's a major river—much broader and deeper than those we've crossed so far. Everything has to be taken out of each wagon, the wagons taken apart and tarred, and then all the pieces and supplies loaded back into the beds. We'll stretch a sturdy rope across the river, wrap it around a tree on the far side, and then, one wagon at a time, we'll tie the rope to the ends of the wagon and pull it to the other side." Jack shook his head. "It's a slow process. The man who drowned yesterday lost his footing when he was driving his animals over first."

"Well, God will take care of us," Phillip assured Jack boldly, "but what about you, Mr. Montgomery . . . do you have a family?"

"No family. I have two wagons and a cattleman, Henry Stowe. Barsina, his wife, is my cook. They were my father's slaves, but my parents are dead. I sold the plantation and promised them their freedom if they would accompany me west."

"That's exceedingly generous of you, Sir."

"I am a generous man—" Jack cleared his throat and ended enigmatically, "when I get what I want." He doffed his hat. "Good-day to you, Reverend. And to you, Miss Lily Ann." His brown eyes challenged Lillian as he tugged the mud-spattered kerchief up over his nose.

As Jack disappeared into the mist, Lillian shrugged off the uncomfortable feelings his presence had roused in her; she'd think about them later.

Watching Phillip step up on the wagon tongue, she said, "That poor woman and her children; how very sad." Her arms tightened around her quilt and she unconsciously hugged herself. "Will we make it safely across, do you think?"

"Don't worry, Lill," Phillip assured her cheerfully, leaping up to the spring seat. "Lots of folk have gone before us. They've made it just fine—and we will too." He turned to look at her with searching eyes. "I meant it when I told Mr. Montgomery that God will take care of us." His brow furrowed. "You do believe that, don't you, Lill?"

"Of course I do, Phillip. You know I do," she affirmed stoutly.

"Well, then let's not be worrying. We are God's servants, here to help others. There's no need to be downcast."

Phillip's confidence boosted Lillian's spirits. Releasing her quilt, she spread it over her hope chest and then settled on it, thinking how fitting it was that she sat on the word **TRUST**. As she mused over that word, embroidered in green floss and surrounded by a circle of ivy print pieces, she wondered if the missionary society ladies had remembered to pray for her.

* * *

The tragedy that had befallen the returning wagon train discouraged many of the travelers. When the Scranton party reached the swollen Kaw River, the violence of its swift, muddy currents so shocked and frightened the families of twenty-three wagons that they chose to turn back.

Although there was an old ferryboat downstream, the proprietor charged a high price per wagon and the ferry was rumored to be unsafe. So, after waiting over a week for the river to go down and the currents to slow a bit, the parties in front of the Scranton train headed across. When it was finally their turn, the remaining thirty-nine wagons were unloaded near the river, the wheels and hardware were removed, and all the seams, inside and out, were caulked with resin and tar—a very messy job—and then the wagon beds were reloaded.

Everyone watched as the stock went first. Those men with horses rounded up the cattle and herded them toward the river. The animals that reached the water first tried to turn around and run; they lowed and butted each other, some even stumbled. But eventually, with the help of the horsemen's stinging whips, they took the plunge—and all at once they were swimming. Their heads bobbed, they bawled and snorted, but the horsemen rode into the river and formed a boundary on either side of them that steered them in the right direction.

Herding the livestock across the Kaw took most of

the morning, but success had everyone breathing a sigh of relief. When they stopped for a short, early nooning, several men suggested they press on and not take a break. Between mouthfuls of bread and cheese, Phillip reported Mr. Scranton's decision to Lillian: "Our families and supplies are too precious to set ourselves up for tragedy because our strength is depleted."

It was Phillip's turn to lead the wagons, which meant the Denbeigh wagon would be pulled across the Kaw first. Lillian's stomach had felt so queasy that she'd sat on a crate of hymnals, hugging her quilt while she watched. When lunch time came, she was so nervous she couldn't choke down more than a couple of mouthfuls. Phillip, on the other hand, ate every bite of his meal and finished hers as well. He didn't appear to be worried at all, and Lillian wished she had his calm assurance.

When Mr. Scranton, accompanied by Jack Montgomery, walked up to their wagon, Lillian knew the time had come to be brave—but she'd never felt more fearful in her life. Clutching her quilt, she pressed the word **COURAGE** to her chest and sent up a quick prayer. *Help, God!*

Phillip attached a thick rope to the rear of their wagon bed. Jack wrapped the rope around a nearby sturdy tree and then fearlessly guided his chestnut stallion across the swiftly moving river. Several men on horseback accompanied him. When the rope had been looped around a tree trunk on the opposite bank, one of the men rode back with the free end and helped

Phillip tie it securely to the front of their wagon.

Lillian felt the anxious stares of everyone in the train when Phillip came to lift her into their wagon bed. As he bent down to pick her up, she clutched her quilt in a death grip, held her breath, and squeezed her eyes shut.

When she was safely settled, she heard Mr. Scranton call out, "Ready!"

She opened her eyes just as Phillip pushed off and swung himself into the wagon bed. The men on each bank hauled on the rope. The wagon slowly slid into the river. Risking a glance at the rushing water, Lillian's stomach shot into her throat and she thought she was going to be sick. She gulped air, convulsively pinching her quilt with tense fingers of one hand and gripping the side of the wagon with the other.

The wagon bounced. It dipped and creaked. Water shot into the air, showering them with spray as the rushing current threatened to capsize the wagon. Lillian bit her lips, determined not to embarrass herself. Her fingers squeezed the side of the wagon until they felt frozen to the board. She more begged than prayed a silent prayer, *"Oh, please, God, help us get safely across."*

Her stomach seemed permanently lodged in her throat as the wagon rocked up and down and jerked from side to side.

Then suddenly, she was jolted forward in an abrupt bump. The wagon plowed into the mud on the opposite riverbank and scraped to a stop. With shaking fingers

Lillian pulled her handkerchief from her cuff and wiped the spray from her face. When she peeked with one eye, she saw that Phillip had already jumped out of the wagon bed. His boots sank in the mud and made sucking sounds as he pulled them out to take the next steps, but he didn't seem to notice.

Phillip turned to her and held out his arms. She tried to stand, but her legs wobbled and she sank back down. Phillip leaned in and picked her up, quilt and all, and carried her over the mud.

Safely on dry ground, she swirled her quilt around her shoulders and huddled into it, struggling to calm her frayed emotions. Sinking to the grass, she fixed her gaze on Phillip as he moved back to the water's edge and then assisted Jack and his crew in dragging their wagon to high, dry ground.

"Well done, Miss Lily Ann," Jack called back to her as he headed down to the riverbank. As he mounted his horse and headed back across the river with the rope, Lillian closed her eyes and rested her head on her knees. There was no turning back now; the Kaw was the final boundary between any semblance of civilization and the vast, uncharted new world.

* * *

All the livestock had been accounted for and the reassembled wagons stood in their customary circle. Guarding the wagons and livestock against wolves, Indian raids, and unscrupulous thieves who reputedly preyed on the vulnerable wagon trains, the men rotated in shifts to patrol the outer perimeter of the camp. The weather had grown increasingly pleasant in the days since the downpour, and that, along with the safe crossing of the Kaw, had boosted the travelers' spirits.

Tonight, nearly everyone had gathered in the wagon circle, where a central campfire's leaping flames illuminated the common area. Children shouted, happy to run and play freely in the lush, abundant grass. Adults and older youth chatted or sang along to the lively tunes scratched out on fiddles and banjos or whistled on recorders that folks had brought with them. Lillian hummed along as she and Phillip progressed around the circle, socializing with their fellow travelers.

As the fiddlers segued from "Old Dan Tucker" into "Oh, Susannah," a handful of free-spirited folks kicked up their heels in enthusiastic—if not particularly skillful—folk dancing. Lillian, her eyes shining as brightly as the fireflies flitting in the prairie darkness, grabbed her husband's hand and tugged him toward the dancers. "Oh, Phillip, how exciting! I just love to dance."

She felt Phillip freeze, silent, unmoving. Then his hand pumped hers spasmodically.

"What? Why are you looking at me like that?" She stopped, waited, a bewildered expression on her face.

"Ah . . . I guess we've never had . . . an occasion to discuss . . ."

She broke into his stammering hesitation, "You don't . . . think . . . dancing is . . . appropriate for the minister and his wife . . ." Her voice trailed away into a mournful little sigh. Then she straightened her shoulders and summoned a shaky smile. "I wouldn't want to do anything unsuitable or inappropriate." When Phillip pulled her close with a whispered, "Thank you," she leaned her head against his shoulder.

In the next moment, Betsey's voice calling out a cheerful greeting attracted their attention. Together, they turned and watched her approach. Baby Elizabeth rested on one hip. Evan and Emily tagged along, darting after fireflies. A tall, willowy young woman, largely pregnant, walked beside Betsey on one side. On the other, a tiny, brown-haired girl who looked to be sixteen or seventeen at the most carried a sleeping infant in a cloth sling tied over one shoulder.

Phillip tipped his hat to the women before he moved off to join Mr. Scranton and a group of men a short distance away who were loudly discussing the anticipated hazards of tomorrow's section of the trail.

Elizabeth squirmed and squealed.

Shifting the baby in her arms, Betsey spoke over the child's head. "Lillian, I want you to meet my friends." She turned to the tall, pregnant woman. "This is Sally Mae Newcomb. Sally Mae and I have been friends for years."

Lillian smiled at the young woman whose upturned nose gave her face a perpetually cheerful expression. "I'm pleased to make your acquaintance."

Sally Mae nodded. "I stood up with Betsey when she and Lewis got married."

"That's right!" Betsey exclaimed, her blue eyes

lighting with memories. "How time flies. Now I have three children," she smiled at Lillian and then nodded toward her pregnant friend, "and Tom and Sally Mae are expecting their first. I'm guessing he'll be a red-head. Like his mama." The look she exchanged with Sally Mae said this baby was welcome indeed.

Betsey turned to the brown-haired girl. "And this is Rebecca Lawson and her new baby, Milton—junior, after his daddy."

Lillian beamed at her. "Ooh, I do so want a baby." Longing oozed from every pore.

"Come by and visit any time we're stopped. If he's awake, you can hold him," Rebecca offered shyly.

Evan darted around Lillian and mischievously jerked one of Elizabeth's dangling bare feet. When the baby wailed loudly and her eyes welled up with big tears, Betsey focused on her children.

"We're excited about the baby," Sally Mae told Lillian, wrinkling up her nose and setting her freckles in motion, "but I'm glad they arrive only one at a time." She chuckled as she smoothed her hands over her distended abdomen. "Look at me—and I still have several weeks to go."

Betsey restored order among her little brood in time to hear Sally Mae's last comment. "Don't worry, Sal, your baby will be right on time—what with all the walking you've been doing."

She changed the subject without stopping for a breath, "Lewis says walking saves the oxen, but it sure has worn out my shoes." She sighed, adding, "The soles of my sturdiest pair already have holes in several places. It's too bad we can't go barefooted like the children."

The women exchanged a wistful glance; a genteel lady would never be seen in public without her legs and feet properly encased in stockings and shoes.

"In one of the letters we read before we left Warrensburg, a missionary wrote that some women have started wearing baggy cotton pantaloons—bloomers, they're called—with only a short skirt over them." Rebecca shook her head, "I can't imagine what my mother would think of that!"

"Nor mine," Lillian agreed, rolling her eyes.

Betsey chuckled. "Well, I don't have a mother to approve or disapprove, but I don't think our church ladies would have thought wearing pants in any shape or form was acceptable—although I could be tempted to put them on my Emily; she does so like to run and tumble, and I'm constantly having to remind her to keep her skirt down and hold her knees together."

Lillian nodded and then sniffed the air. "Mmm," she savored the aroma of roasting meat wafting toward them. "That reminds me—I meant to ask Phillip to lift the lid of our trunk."

She explained to Sally Mae and Rebecca, "I have a tin of recipes in our trunk that Nora, our family cook back home, sent with me. Betsey and I are hoping we'll discover some ways to make our meals more interesting."

"I could use some help, too," Sally Mae said, expressing a desire to be included.

Rebecca nodded. "Me, too."

Their eagerness prompted Lillian to offer, "We'll let you know when we're going to look through them."

Elizabeth yawned, drawing Betsey's attention back to her children. "It's getting late. Time for me to put these babies to bed." She called out, "Evan, hold Emily's hand, please."

"Sally Mae, Rebecca, it was nice to meet you both," Lillian said, nodding a farewell to her new acquaintances. "I'll see you in the morning, Betsey."

Lifting her skirt and petticoat, Lillian turned away. Studying the ground to avoid stepping into holes hidden by the darkness, she moved cautiously, so focused that she didn't hear the approaching footsteps.

A hand touched her shoulder from behind. "Miss Lily Ann?"

"Oh!" Lillian jumped and cried out. "You startled me," she reproached, dropping her skirt. She clapped her hands to her cheeks to cool the flush suffusing her face. What was there about Jack Montgomery that made her feel so flustered?

"Where are you going in such a hurry?" Jack's mellow drawl sent shivers up her spine.

"To find Phillip." She was instantly irritated at sounding breathless and defensive.

"Ah, yes. The preacher." There was a momentary pause. Jack's dark eyes seemed to bore into hers. "How did a passionate little thing like you get hooked up with such a do-gooder?"

Lillian gaped, then she sputtered, "Passio—!" She

sucked in her breath. "You've got nerve." She dashed away from Jack, heedless of the terrain.

"Case in point about your passionate nature, Miss Lily Ann." He was laughing at her; it was in his voice.

Her right foot plunged into a hole concealed in the long grass. Pain shot like lightning through her ankle as she crashed to the ground. She bit her lower lip, struggling to keep from crying out.

Jack was instantly on his knees beside her.

"Just leave me alone, Mr. Montgomery," Lillian burst out angrily, glaring at him. "This is your fault."

Before she could get back on her feet and recapture her dignity, Jack scooped her up in his arms and hugged her close to his chest—far too close for Lillian's peace of mind. The smell of leather and spices filled her senses, making the simple act of breathing suddenly much more difficult. Desperate to get away, she strained against his arms.

Jack laughed softly, a rich, chest-based rumble.

"Put me down," Lillian demanded, kicking her feet and squirming.

But Jack's strong arms held her firmly in place as his chuckle rumbled again. "Not until I see you safely delivered to your wagon. Your Reverend is over there," he jerked his head toward the campfire, "visiting with Miss Vargas." Implication filled his pause before he observed, "I think you would not want me to carry you to him just now."

"Let me go," she hissed, again struggling to wrench free.

"Hold still, you little wildcat. Do you want to draw attention to yourself?"

Jack was right; she did not wish to appear before Phillip and the sensual Miss Vargas in such a humiliated state. She stopped fighting and snapped ungraciously, "All right, take me to my wagon." She ducked her head, hoping no one would recognize her.

When Jack deposited her on the spring seat, she ground out through her clenched teeth, "I won't be thanking you. If it weren't for you, I wouldn't have stepped in that hole in the first place. Now go away and leave me alone." She was trembling, holding herself together through sheer willpower.

"I'll go away—for now, but I won't be leaving you alone," Jack promised in a low voice before he vanished into the shadows.

Lillian scrubbed at her face where Jack's warm breath had touched her cheek. "Infernal audacity! How dare he be so bold?" she scolded, scrambling into the wagon. "And me a married woman!"

Dropping to the floor, she massaged her ankle until the throbbing began to subside.

Still too upset to change into her night clothes, she wrapped up in her quilt and settled against her hope chest, intending to wait for Phillip. Within minutes, she was asleep.

Phillip's boots thumped against the spring seat as he climbed into the wagon. Startled, Lillian sat up abruptly as his body filled the opening between the flaps.

"Phillip?" she whispered in a thin, shaky voice.

"So sorry to wake you," he apologized.

She pushed her hair away from her face, her tone bordering on accusation. "Why were you gone so long?"

"Ah—I was talking with Miss Vargas. She has so many questions about what I believe. And what I'll be doing in Oregon."

"Oh, really?" Her tone was spiky. After all, she'd seen Desiree Vargas up close.

"Yes, really." Phillip's surprise echoed between them. "I thought you'd be pleased that I had such a great opportunity to share my faith."

Instantly ashamed of her pique, Lillian quickly apologized. "Of course I am, Phillip. I don't know what's ailing me." Jack Montgomery was what was ailing her, and she knew it. And adding the sultry Desiree into the equation—oh, why did she feel so irritated and jealous?

Phillip's curled fingers tenderly smoothed the softness of her cheek. "Are you feeling all right?"

Tears sprang into her eyes. "No. I sprained my ankle in the field." She tried to make light of her accident, "Mr. Montgomery happened to be nearby, so he carried me to the wagon. I didn't change into my nightclothes because I was waiting for you."

"Oh, my dear. Come here." Phillip cradled her in his arms. "There, there," he soothed, wiping her damp cheeks. "Is your ankle going to be all right?"

"It is now," she whispered, comforted by his embrace, his warm kisses, and his familiar sage scent.

CHAPTER FOUR

Bigger and closer than back home—and hotter; that's how the sun felt, beating down on Lillian's head and shoulders.

Soon after leaving Independence, the Scranton Party had passed strange rock outcroppings: Courthouse Rock and Jailhouse Rock, rising up side-by-side, and then Chimney Rock, looking like a haystack with a pole sticking up through its top and visible for forty miles in both directions along the trail.

The broad, shading oak trees that dotted the Kansas flatland had disappeared, along with the profuse array of wildflowers ranging from violets to daisies to geraniums. The mockingbirds and meadowlarks that sang their hearts out and cheered the travelers had been replaced by an occasional mournful owl.

They had moved on from the Kansas prairie through the sandy, grass-covered plains of Nebraska and into Wyoming, where the intense heat made breathing almost unbearable and the barren land reminded everyone of how far they still must travel to reach verdant Oregon.

Lillian thought about the lonely sod shanties and rude shacks they'd passed since leaving Independence, about the land that had become treeless and flat in every direction, and wondered that any right-thinking person would be content to live in this forsaken place when they could move on and settle in the paradise that was Oregon.

Four days ago they'd passed an abandoned Indian village—just a couple of teepee skeletons and fire pits. Mr. Scranton said they'd been "relocated." Lillian wondered what that meant and made a mental note to ask Phillip.

Prairie dog towns, mounds of heaped earth with holes in the center, scattered out on either side of the trail as far as one could see. The small creatures would sit up and bark at the travelers, their squeaky little voices chiding furiously before they nose-dived into their burrows. At first Lillian thought they were cute. But as the days passed, their sporadic scolding grew irritating, and Lillian found herself scolding back, "Be quiet, you silly little beasts."

With the growing intensity of the heat, Mr. Scranton repeatedly cautioned everyone to be on the lookout for rattlesnakes, warning that the slithery reptiles slept through the winter, but with the arrival of hot weather, they left their dens in rocky places to sun themselves and hunt for food. In fresh skins of velvety black, or yellow with brown bands, and shaking their new rattles in warning, rattlesnakes moved quickly and their strikes usually proved fatal. Furthermore, he advised them to keep their faces to the wind when relieving themselves, collecting buffalo dung off-trail, or hunting, alert for the peculiar vapor given off by the rattlers' scaly skins in warm sunlight.

Lewis Harmon did indeed love to hunt, and the antelope and buffalo that roamed the prairie offered prime opportunities for him to exercise his skill. Milton Lawson frequently joined him, and the two men occasionally shared the meat they brought back with their friends, which provided a welcome change from bacon or jerky.

Lillian saw Milton approach Lewis during the nooning. Within a few minutes, guns in hand, the two friends headed off toward a herd of buffalo, an undulating brown mass on a broad slope in the distance.

Less than fifteen minutes later, while Lillian was sweeping out the bed of their wagon, a gun-shot startled her. She smiled and immediately began planning what she would serve with an anticipated cut of fresh buffalo meat.

But distant shouts interrupted her salivating thoughts. The ground shook, rocking the wagon and rattling the tools hanging on the outside. When she stuck her head out of the wagon, she could see the buffalo herd stampeding over a rise. And then she saw them; two small specks—Lewis Harmon and Milton Lawson were on the ground. Oh, she did so hope that meant they had felled a mighty beast. But just as she drew back to return to her sweeping, Lewis leaped up and began waving wildly and shouting, "Help! Help!"

Jack Montgomery and Tom Newcomb grabbed their guns and raced toward the two hunters. In a matter of minutes nearly all the members of the wagon train stood outside their wagons. Shading their eyes from the sun, they stared at Jack Montgomery as he turned around and dashed back across the prairie toward the Lawson wagon. Carrying Milton Lawson between them on their shoulders, Tom and Lewis followed at a slower pace.

News traveled quickly: Milton had been bitten a rattlesnake. By the time the men got him to his wagon, his leg had swelled to twice its normal size, discoloration had set in, and his body was sweating profusely in its desperate attempt to throw off the poison. Lewis's account was the talk around the campfire that night. Dark looks and throaty whispers intimated that Milton may not recover.

Phillip repeated the story to Lillian in every bit as much detail as if he'd been there himself. "Milton was over a hundred paces ahead of Lewis, chasing a straggling buffalo calf. He raised his gun and closed one eye. But just when he had the calf lined up in his sight, he stepped on something that moved. His foot slipped and he fell, and his finger caught on the trigger, shooting off his gun. He hit his head so hard on a rock that it rendered him unable to yell or move. The rattler reared, shook her rattles, and struck out, biting him in his left thigh. He said it stung like fire."

Lillian shivered at Phillip's vivid description.

"Lewis didn't see the rattler—it must have slithered away—so he thought Milton had tripped and banged his head. But when Milton regained his senses and explained what had happened, Lewis ripped the leg of his friend's breeches to expose the fang holes. Immediately, Lewis put his mouth over the bloody red marks and sucked hard and then spit. But even though he repeated the process again and again, Milton's leg started to swell—and when he tried to get up, he said his head felt woozy. That's when Lewis shouted for help."

When Phillip paused for a breath, Lillian whispered, "Oh, poor Rebecca. And her with an infant." She clutched Phillip's sleeve. "Milton will recover, won't he?"

Phillip frowned and was slow to reply, finally conceding, "I—don't know." Seeing the startled expression on Lillian's face, he quickly added, "Dr. Murphy did say it was good that Lewis sucked out the poison right away."

"So what can they do now . . . just wait and see?"

"Well, folks offered various remedies." Phillip shook his head disparagingly. "Nanny tea, tobacco leaf poultices, whiskey to ease the pain. But Dr. Murphy said there is no cure." He lowered his voice, "Milton is out of his head; he keeps waving his arms and talking about wrestling a wildcat that's pouncing on him." He caught Lillian's arm, "You will be careful, Lill—when you leave the wagon circle, I mean."

Lillian turned into Phillip's arms, rested her head against his chest, and hugged him tightly, reassured by his steady heartbeat.

In the morning, when the news that paralysis had

set in passed from wagon to wagon, everyone knew it was just a matter of time.

Why, God? Lillian's mind repeated the question. But on a deeper level, she struggled with guilt for her envy of Rebecca and her baby. She picked up her quilt and clutched it to her heart, seeking comfort.

* * *

Lillian shifted on the spring seat and snapped her limp handkerchief at the flies and gnats that swarmed her moist skin, buzzed around her nose, and darted at her eyes—with little success. But pesky insects seemed the least of her worries.

Compounding the heaviness in her heart for Rebecca Lawson's sorrow at the loss of her husband, constant crying echoing from the Harmon wagon for the past three days had left Lillian's nerves as sharply ragged as the frayed edges on her old bonnet. Yesterday she'd still felt sympathy for the children, for how miserable they must feel in the suffocating heat. When they'd stopped at Independence Rock—a gigantic mountain of granite—and everyone had added their names to the collection on its stone face, she'd been sad that Betsey and her children had remained in their wagon.

Today, though, Lillian's patience was worn to a thread. Certain that Betsey must be far more frustrated than her did not make her feel any better. When the wagons stopped for the nooning, Lillian, feeling guilty for her annoyance, admonished herself sternly, *God is watching you, Lillian, and He would not be pleased with your bad attitude. Shame on you. Stop avoiding Betsey and go make yourself useful.*

"I think something is wrong in the Harmon wagon," Lillian voiced her concern to Phillip as she climbed out of the wagon. "I'll see if I can be of help, but maybe you should find Dr. Murray and ask him to come by."

"I think you're right, Lill. I'll go right now."

"Mrs. Denbeigh," Lewis Harmon called, walking toward them. "I overheard you say you could help Betsey. That would be wonderful; she's completely worn out." He ran his hand over his straight brown hair in a despairing gesture. "And I'm just no good with crying children."

Pity rushed through her. "Mr. Harmon, please, why don't you sit here in this patch of shade and rest while Phillip fetches Dr. Murray? I'll check on Betsey."

Lillian approached the back of the Harmon wagon. "Betsey, it's Lillian," she called out loudly to be heard over the crying. "How can I help you?"

The canvas quivered. Then Betsey peered out at her.

Lillian tried to hide her dismay. Betsey was in trouble. Serious trouble. Her normally rosy skin was blotchy and her eyelids were red and swollen; she'd been crying right along with the children.

"Oh, Lillian, I'm so sorry; I'm sure the noise has bothered you," Betsey jiggled Elizabeth in her arms as she attempted to speak over the child's wheezing and wailing, "At first I thought Elizabeth was cutting a tooth, but I've tried everything I did with the other two and nothing has helped; she won't stop crying. So I finally gave her a rag dipped in a bit of honey to suck on—it seemed to help at first, but now she's lethargic and wheezing. She won't nurse," she heaved a weary sigh, "and she's still crying."

There was a loud thud. The wagon rocked and shook. Then frantic, hysterical, deafening shrieks shook the canvas bonnet. Lillian put her hand to her head to ease her throbbing headache.

Betsey turned a haggard face inward; she gave a sharp cry and slumped down on a crate as if her legs had turned to custard.

Lillian fought the urge to run away. Far away. And fast.

But she determinedly reminded herself of her duty: *We are here to help, and God won't be pleased if I shirk my responsibility.* She clambered up the back, swung one leg over the backboard, and lost her balance, toppling into the echo chamber that was the Harmon wagon.

Clenching her teeth on a groan, she lifted her head. Her eyes landed on Emily. The little girl was bouncing up and down on a large crate and screeching hysterically. Her dimpled arms beat the air and her small hands flapped wildly. Panic dilated her blue eyes.

Beside her, Evan was bent in half, tugging to free his right leg that had become wedged between two crates. His knee was distended backwards. And his bloodcurdling screams, too big for his tiny body, ricocheted around the inside of the wagon like punctuating drumbeats to Emily's descant.

One look at Betsey told Lillian that her friend would be no help; frozen in shock, Betsey stared blankly at the floor.

Lillian got to her feet, grabbed Emily by her shoulder, and shook her lightly to interrupt the squealing cycle. At Lillian's touch, the child's eyes rolled back in her head and she collapsed on the crate, limp as a rag doll without its stuffing.

"Oh, God, help!" Lillian muttered. When she saw the little girl's chest rise and fall, she turned her attention to Evan.

A quick glance assured her there was adequate space to move the heavy crate; that is, if she proved strong enough to budge it. She dropped to her knees, braced her feet on the adjacent carton, and leaned forward. Holding her breath, she pushed with all her might.

The shrill screeching caused by the crate scraping against the wagon bed sent slivers of pain shooting from Lillian's ears down her neck and into her shoulders. Then—yes! The crate moved a couple of inches. Just enough. She scrambled to her feet and squatted behind Evan, hooking her palms under his armpits. But his slight appearance was deceiving—he was heavier than he looked. And his continued screaming and flailing didn't help the situation. Or her nerves.

"Urrrr." Lillian's desperate groan roiled between her teeth as she yanked Evan upward with all her strength. But her surge of elation when his leg came free only lasted a heartbeat before the momentum of his weight threw her off balance; she landed on her back with Evan on top of her, slamming her shoulder blades down against the crate. The air left her lungs in a whoosh.

Thrusting Evan off her chest, Lillian gasped for breath and sat up, ready to rejoice in her victory. Evan was free! And he was silent.

She looked down—and her heart sank to her shoes. Evan's knee was not right.

In the next moment he resumed screaming—even louder than before, it seemed, since his mouth was closer to her face.

Lillian rolled to her knees and firmly but as gently as she could manage, maneuvered Evan's small body onto his side, propping his back against a crate.

"Dr. Murray will be here soon," she soothed—for her own benefit, she realized, since there was no way Evan could hear her over his screams.

Surprised by the tears dripping off her chin, Lillian scraped at them impatiently and cast a frantic glance at Betsey. Alarmed by her friend's still-vacant, wandering eyes, she suddenly feared for baby Elizabeth's safety. She struggled to her feet and impulsively plucked the wheezing infant from Betsey's lap.

Where, oh, where was Phillip? Why hadn't he returned with Dr. Murray? Evan needed help. Emily needed help. Elizabeth needed help. Betsey needed help. *She* needed help. Now!

Lillian staggered to the back of the wagon, off-balance due to the unaccustomed weight of a child pressed to her chest. "I've got to find the doctor, Betsey. I'll be right back." She hoped her friend understood.

Shifting Elizabeth into the crook of her right arm, Lillian pivoted sideways and clutched the back of the wagon with her left hand. Keeping her eyes on Evan and Betsey, she eased one leg at a time over the backboard, carefully managing her skirt. Facing into the wagon, Lillian balanced on her toes on the ledge, preparing to leap backwards to the ground. But fear and stress took their toll. As her whole body started to shake, she lost her grip and fell backwards. Instinct made her curl her arms protectively around the baby.

"Help!" she cried feebly, even though she knew there was no one to hear.

Strong arms caught her and held her steady. "Whoa, there. What's all this fuss about?"

Jack Montgomery. Not again!

Steeling herself against the temptation to lean her weary head against his brawny chest, Lillian ground her teeth together and pulled away from the smell of leather and spices. And answered more sharply than he deserved, "We need a doctor. Evan's leg is broken, Emily fainted, the baby is sick, and Betsey's in shock." Her voice quavered despite her determination to keep it steady.

"Are *you* all right?" He said it as if he knew she wanted to run away and never come back.

Hoping she sounded more confident than she felt, Lillian avoided his eyes and asserted curtly, "Of course I'm all right. Why wouldn't I be?"

"Sh-sh-sh," she whispered near Elizabeth's ear as she shifted the whimpering baby from one arm to the other and abruptly reminded herself of her duty. *It will never do to let Jack see me as weak; that would give him all the more reason to scoff at my faith. No, God expects me to be strong.*

"I've brought Dr. Murray," Phillip announced in a breathless voice, rounding the end of the wagon. A white-haired gentleman hurried after him, carrying a black medical bag in his gnarled, brown-spotted hand.

Lewis Harmon, still looking lost and disoriented, struggled to his feet from his shaded spot beside the wagon and staggered forward. When he swayed and nearly fell, Phillip caught his arm. "Here, Lewis, lean on me. Dr. Murray will take care of everything." He guided Lewis back to the wagon and rested against it beside his friend.

Appointing himself Dr. Murray's assistant, Jack swung himself up into the Harmon wagon. "This way, Sir," he offered, reaching his hand down for the doctor's medical bag. Dr. Murray handed the black bag up to Jack and then hoisted himself over the backboard.

Unaccustomed to carrying a baby, Lillian arched her back and shifted Elizabeth to redistribute the child's weight. She turned to Phillip and whispered, "My arms are aching. If you would fetch my quilt from our wagon and lay it here," she pointed to a narrow strip of shade beside the Harmon wagon, "I could put the baby on it."

Phillip sped toward their wagon, leaped up on the wagon tongue, and climbed inside. Returning shortly with his wife's quilt, he spread it on the grass in the wagon's shadow.

Lillian knelt and settled Elizabeth's curled up little body on the blanket. The infant's pale cheek covered the word **REST** embroidered in bright blue floss. Bluebells in the circle of flowered fabric banded her head like a halo. Smoothing the baby's hand-stitched cotton dress over her tiny form, Lillian begged in a low voice, "Please, God, give this family rest."

Inside the wagon, Dr. Murray checked Emily's pulse. In his Scott's-burred English he reported that her heartbeat was steady and that her skin color appeared normal. She would likely be fine when she woke up.

Calling down to Phillip, Jack passed along Dr. Murray's instructions to remove Emily from the wagon and place her in the shade beside Elizabeth.

Betsey stirred when the men lifted Emily. "Wha-what's happening? Where's my baby?"

When Jack explained that Lillian was caring for Elizabeth, Betsey sprang toward the back of the wagon. Phillip, leaning against the wagon, heard her as she started to clamber over the backboard. Immediately, he offered her his hand and assisted her to the ground. When she saw her daughters lying motionless on Lillian's quilt, she darted toward them.

Alert to Betsey's movements, Lillian leaped to her feet and intercepted her friend, whispering, "They're both sleeping, Betsey. Why don't you get some rest, too?" She guided Betsey toward the closest wagon wheel, where the exhausted woman slumped down, closed her eyes, and let her head fall back against the wheel rim.

Jack popped his head out from the rear of the Harmon wagon and called to Phillip. In a low voice he explained that Evan's knee was out of joint and that putting it back into place would undoubtedly be painful, so Phillip should be prepared to comfort the family members when the boy began screaming again.

Phillip passed the warning to Lewis, who sank to the grass in the shade beside his wife. Lillian overheard Phillip's caution and knelt beside Elizabeth, placing her hand on the baby's tummy to provide comfort and reassurance should her brother's crying disturb her sleep.

Phillip squatted beside Emily just as Evan let out a blood-chilling scream. Betsey scrunched her eyes tightly closed and clapped her hands over her ears as she pulled her knees up close to her body. Emily stirred, and Phillip instantly lifted her into his arms, cradling her against his shoulder as he shifted to sit cross-legged. With her flaxen head burrowed into his neck, Phillip stroked the little girl's back in soothing circles until Evan's screams finally eased to ragged hiccoughs.

Just as everyone started to relax, Jack poked his head out the back of the wagon. "Mr. Harmon?"

"Coming," Lewis replied. He scrambled to his feet and dashed around the end of the wagon.

In a low, firm voice, Jack said, "Dr. Murray is wondering if your wife would be up to sitting with Evan. His leg will be all right, but he needs his mother."

Scraping his hands together nervously, Lewis returned to the quilt. He squatted beside Betsey and gently eased one hand from her cheek. "Bets," he whispered, "can you hear me?" When Betsey's eyes came into focus on her husband's face, he said, "Evan needs you."

Betsey grabbed her husband's arm, her eyes wide with anxiety, and stuttered, "Is—is his leg going to—be all right?"

"Yes, Bets, Evan's going to be fine. But the doctor wants you to sit with him." Lewis squeezed her hand and then pulled her to her feet. With his arm around his wife's waist, Lewis walked with Betsey to the back of the wagon.

Lillian fanned Elizabeth with her handkerchief to chase the flies off her face and neck, but as she watched the baby, her uneasiness grew; the child's breathing seemed shallow and labored and her small body twitched involuntarily.

"Dr. Murray," she sprang up and ran to him as soon as he was back on the ground, "while you're here, would you mind checking on the baby?" She knew her concern was evident on her face.

When Dr. Murray reached the quilt, Phillip, still holding Emily in his arms, shifted to his knees and rose to his feet. Then he stepped aside to give the doctor more room beside the baby. While Phillip, Lillian, and Lewis looked on, Dr. Murray checked and re-checked Elizabeth's pulse. He pressed his ear to her chest to listen to her heartbeat. Then he pushed up her eyelids.

When the baby didn't respond, Lillian bit her lip and looked away—and met Jack's gaze head-on; he was standing on the ground with his back propped against the rear corner of the wagon, watching her. Instantly vexed, she returned her gaze to Elizabeth.

Dr. Murray's grave expression alerted them to the possibility of bad news. "Ach. This bonny wee bairn . . ." He rubbed his chin thoughtfully. "What hae she been eating?"

Startled, Lillian stammered, "Wha—what do you mean? Betsey nurses her . . ." When he shook his head and frowned, Lillian added, "Elizabeth was cutting a tooth; Betsey said she dipped a cloth in honey and let her suck on it." When the doctor's frown deepened, Lillian puzzled, "But honey's good for us . . . isn't it?"

Dr. Murray's eyes narrowed, "Not for babies, it isn't." A grim expression settled on his face but no one was prepared for his shocking pronouncement, "'t'is only a matter of time noo."

He stood up and addressed Lillian, "Ye be staying on close by." He jerked his head toward the wagon, "I thole they'll be in mighty need of ye." As he spoke, the tiny, perfect little body gave one last convulsive shudder and then lay still.

Lillian's face lost all color.

Jack swore under his breath.

Then after a pause that seemed to last a lifetime, Lillian wilted to her knees. The little gathering watched as she slowly eased backward onto the grass. She caught up a corner of her quilt, lifted the orange marigolds surrounding the word COMFORT, and slowly folded them over the infant's body.

But in spite of her apparent outward calm, Lillian's thoughts swirled in anguished turmoil. *God, how could You let this happen? These people love you. And Elizabeth was just an innocent baby!*

As Dr. Murray turned away, Lewis caught his arm and stumbled into him. The doctor steadied him. They spoke briefly in hushed voices.

Snapping whips, lowing oxen, and creaking wagons that started moving up ahead reminded the little group caught in tragedy's web that time and the rest of the world forever move forward.

With Lewis clinging to his arm, Dr. Murray returned to the tragic scene. His Scotch frugality afforded no flowery words as he reported Lewis's concern. "Mr. Harmon is a'feared to tell his wife the bairn is dead." He looked straight at Lillian. "He wonders if ye'd be tellin' her, Mrs. Denbeigh."

Lillian suppressed a groan even as she agreed softly, "Yes, I'll tell her." *Why me, God?*

"And would ye allow the wee body be put to riding in your wagon?" Dr. Murray shifted his medical bag from one hand to the other. "Mr. Harmon believes his wife would be of a peace if she kens the bairn is wi' ye."

Lillian felt Jack's eyes on her. She wasn't too sure how she felt about a loving God at the moment but her determination to hide her struggle from Jack made her answer firmly, "Of course. That is certainly the best thing to do. And I can watch over Emily, too." She motioned for Phillip to move the still-sleeping girl into their wagon.

As Lillian bent to wrap the infant's body more securely in her quilt, Jack appeared beside her. "Let me," he whispered gruffly. Their eyes met and held in a moment of shared grief before she dropped hers to the tragic bundle she transferred to his arms.

"You're a brave woman, Miss Lily Ann," Jack said as he turned away.

Stone-faced, Lillian followed Jack to her wagon. She stood behind him as he raised the quilt and its sad contents to Phillip, who had already settled Emily on their bedding on the wagon floor.

Jack dropped his arms and swung around abruptly, crashing into Lillian. He caught her as she stumbled and pulled her tight against his chest to steady her.

Held fast, her face pressed into Jack's shoulder, Lillian breathed in the scent of leather, freshly laundered linen, and something else—not from a bottle. She recoiled, gasping for air. As her head jerked up, her eyes collided with Phillip's troubled gaze. Pulling free from Jack, she stammered awkwardly, "Th-thank you for catching me, Mr. Montgomery."

Lillian stepped around Jack and raised her hand to her husband. "Sweetheart, please help me up; I'll stay with Emily." Phillip grabbed her hand and steadied her as she climbed over the backboard.

Inside the wagon, reality closed in on Lillian. Her anxious gaze darted to the corners.

Sensing her apprehension, Phillip reassured her, "I hid the—the quilt behind the crate of hymnals."

Lillian's worried gaze flew to the crate in the corner. When she saw that not even an edge of the quilt stuck out, she heaved a relieved sigh. "Oh, thank you, Phillip. You are so thoughtful." She sank to the floor beside Emily.

"I love you, Lill—and don't you forget it," he growled, confirming Lillian's suspicion that he deemed Jack's embrace inappropriate.

She clutched at her husband's sleeve, desperate to explain. "Phillip, Mr. Montgomery almost knocked me over. He was only trying to help me regain my balance." Her voice dropped to a whisper, "You have no reason to be jealous."

Cupping her cheek with his hand, Phillip bent over and kissed her. She returned his kiss, breathing an intense, "I love you, Phillip."

Emily slept all afternoon. Lillian fanned the child's face until her arms grew tired and her eyes felt too heavy to hold open. She curled up beside the sleeping child and took a nap.

CHAPTER FIVE

Lillian woke to the tickle of little fingers poking at her eyelids. She opened her eyes and met Emily's curious gaze with startled bewilderment. Then she remembered: She was watching Emily for Betsey.

And the baby.

She sat up with a start. *Elizabeth is dead!*

Light-headed, she sank back to the floor. *I have to tell Betsey that her baby is dead.* Her chest felt so tight she could hardly breathe.

"I want my mama." Emily's plaintive childish treble brought Lillian back to the present.

"When we stop, in a little while, you can go to your mama," Lillian cajoled in her most indulgent tone.

Emily's lower lip quivered. Tears popped into her big blue eyes and she began to whine, "I want my mama!"

Squeezing the back of her neck to relieve her tension, Lillian forced a smile and reprimanded herself: *I must do what God expects of me—and that is to be patient and gentle.*

"Come here, Sweetie." Lillian reached for the child, "You can sit on my lap until we stop, and then I'll take you to your mama." But Emily's small body grew stiff and her cries grew louder. Giant teardrops rolled down her cheeks. And in spite of Lillian's soothing words, the child wailed intermittently for the next hour and a half.

By the time the wagons finally circled for the night, Lillian, weary and exasperated, scooped up the child and said curtly, "Come on, Miss Emily. Let's go find your mama."

Poking her head out the front of the wagon, Lillian spoke to Phillip in a tense, strained voice as she thrust the little girl toward him, "Here, hold Emily until I can get down. I'm taking her to her mother." While Lillian climbed onto the bench and dropped to the ground, Emily cried and squirmed in Phillip's arms.

Betsey looked out the back of her wagon just as Phillip handed the child down to Lillian. Her face broke into a wide smile. "Come to Mama, little Emmy," she called, extending her arms.

"Mama! Mama!" Emily's pathetic little cry rose in relief as Lillian lifted the child to her mother.

"Oh, Lillian, how can I thank you? Evan's leg is going to be all right, and I got a wonderful nap." She settled Emily on her hip and rocked her back and forth, crooning, "Mama's got you, little Emmy. Mama's got you."

Safe in her mother's arms, Emily quickly recovered her normal, sunny attitude and began wriggling to get down. Betsey lowered the child to her feet and watched her scoot out of sight into the wagon.

Lillian looked up at her friend, uncertain how to say what had to be said. *Why me, God? Why, oh, why couldn't Lewis be strong enough to tell his wife? Of course I want to please You, but this is . . .*

"Is—is Elizabeth still asleep?"

Betsey's amazed question so shocked Lillian that she nearly fainted. She sagged against the wagon.

"Are—are you all right?" Betsey stared down at her.

Lillian threw up a silent, desperate prayer. *O, God, help me!* She lifted her head and tried to form a smile but her mouth just wouldn't cooperate. Forcing words around the lump in her throat, she managed to choke out, "We need to talk . . ." She cleared her throat and tried again. "Betsey, I—ah, I need to talk to you. Could you please come down?"

After a glance into the wagon to check on Evan and Emily, Betsey bent down, speaking as she grasped the backboard, "Lewis said Elizabeth is sleeping in your wagon. Did the doctor give her some medicine?"

Lillian didn't answer immediately. In her peripheral vision she caught sight of Lewis returning from caring for his oxen. When she realized he intended to come to them, she frowned and shook her head and then subtly gestured for him to climb in the front of his wagon to watch the children.

The relief on Lewis's face sent a rush of anger through Lillian's whole body. She felt her face turn hot and she had to bite her tongue to keep from shouting out at him, *"You're such a poor excuse for a man!"*

However, he disappeared around the front of the wagon as Betsey dropped to the ground beside her, immediately sidetracking Lillian's disgust.

Lillian glanced around at the campfires blazing across the darkening meadow. Oh, how she wished for supernatural deliverance from the task at hand. But there was no one to rescue her. There was no escape. She shuddered inwardly and turned to face her friend.

"Betsey, Dr. Murray examined Elizabeth. And he said . . ." she tried again to swallow the lump in her throat. "He said there was n-nothing he could do." How could she tell Betsey that she had caused the death of her own baby by giving her honey?

"Thank you for watching her. She's had a good rest—and so have I." She pressed her palm against the filled-out bodice of her shirtwaist dress. "She'll be waking soon and she'll be hungry."

"Betsey . . ." Lillian's voice sank to a mere whisper, "you don't understand." She placed her hand on her friend's arm. "Elizabeth—Elizabeth is—she's dead, Betsey."

A vague smile softened Betsey's face and she gave a short, indulgent giggle that implied Lillian's mistake was due to inexperience. "No, Lillian, she's just sleeping. If I nurse her, she'll be fine."

Lillian choked back a sob. This was even harder than she'd anticipated. "Betsey, no! Elizabeth is *dead*." She said it firmly.

Betsey's expression grew harsh as she insisted, "Elizabeth just needs her mama. I'm sure of it." She took an aggressive step closer and demanded stridently in Lillian's face, "Are you trying to steal my baby?"

Appalled at the accusation and frightened by the

stark hostility blazing in her friend's eyes, Lillian shrank back, whispering tremulously, "Elizabeth is dead, Betsey."

"You can't have my baby. Elizabeth is mine." Betsey's voice rose to a shrill pitch, "Give me my baby!"

Panic swelled in Lillian's chest, but she clenched her fists and held it in, forcing herself to speak quietly, "All right, Betsey. We'll go get your baby."

"I'm coming, Elizabeth. I'm coming," Betsey's frantic voice projected through the dusk as she lurched erratically toward the Denbeigh wagon.

"Wait for me, Betsey," Lillian called out, racing after her friend. She caught up to her at the wagon. Elbowing past the frantic mother, Lillian hoisted herself over the backboard.

Right behind her, Betsey clawed her way up the back of the Denbeigh wagon. Unsteady, hanging on with one hand and swaying crazily, Betsey demanded in a high-pitched screech, "Where is she? Where is my Elizabeth?"

Blinking back her flooding tears, Lillian fumbled around in the dark behind the crate of hymnals until her fingers made contact with the edge of her quilt. Her hands shook as she retrieved the blanket with the tiny body swaddled in its brightly colored bits of fabric. Lillian straightened, clutching her burden to her chest, suddenly paralyzed with terror. How would Betsey react when she discovered that Elizabeth was indeed dead?

When Betsey saw Lillian hugging the quilt and its contents, she lunged forward and forcibly wrenched the bundle from Lillian's arms with both hands. With a shrill exclamation of triumph, she swung around and took a wild, reckless leap.

Stunned, Lillian leaned out and watched her friend falter as she hit the ground, but in the next moment Betsey scrambled to her feet and dashed away. And then it hit Lillian: Emily and Evan would see their mother with the dead baby.

Empowered by a desperate determination to prevent further trauma to the family, Lillian swung her legs over the back of the wagon. She squeezed her eyes closed, hesitated long enough to consider the probability of re-injuring her weak ankle, and then jumped—straight into a pair of strong arms.

"Oh!" she gasped, inhaling a disturbingly familiar masculine scent as her eyes flew open. "Where—what are you doing here?" Lillian demanded of Jack Montgomery.

"I guessed you'd be telling Mrs. Harmon about her baby—and I figured I might be of some help." He stood her on her feet.

His explanation focused Lillian on her reason for jumping in the first place. She grabbed Jack's arm and begged in a low, sharp staccato, "Betsey has Elizabeth—but she won't believe she's dead. Please, you must help me get Evan and Emily out of the Harmon wagon before she realizes the truth."

"Stay here," Jack ordered over his shoulder as he charged toward the Harmon wagon.

Lillian gaped at his back. Then she lifted her chin

and ignored his command. As she approached the rear of the Harmon wagon, Jack's head appeared between the canvas flaps, then his whole body followed. Under each arm he toted a wide-eyed child; they'd been plucked up so quickly they hadn't had time to cry. Jack swung one leg over the backboard and followed it with the second.

"Come, we'll take them to your wagon," he said tersely, dropping to the ground in a deep knee bend beside Lillian.

"What's going on? Those are *my* children!" Lewis barked as he and Phillip appeared out of the shadows.

"Mr. Harmon! I thought—I thought you were in the wagon," Lillian stammered in dismay.

Jack interrupted, his slow drawl diffusing Lewis's tension. "Yes, they are your children, Sir, but your wife is in your wagon trying to—ah—nurse her dead baby. Miss Lily Ann, here, was worried about how these two would fare when your wife realizes the truth."

"Papa, Papa, Papa!" Emily and Evan strained toward their father, their warbling treble voices punctuating Jack's explanation.

Jack handed Emily to Lewis but he held onto Evan. "This young man has to stay off his leg if it's going to heal properly. I'd be happy to see to him for the next couple of days."

Lewis nodded his agreement to Jack's offer. "I should go to Betsey, but what'll I do with Emily?" He gave the little girl a puzzled glance and turned to Lillian. "Mrs. Denbeigh, you don't suppose . . ?"

Jack didn't give Lillian or Phillip a chance to respond. "No, Mr. Harmon," his tone was as hard-edged and cold as a flint blade, "Miss Lily Ann here has had enough for one day." He threw out a suggestion, "How about your wife's friend, Mrs. Newcomb?"

"Ah, yes, good idea." But despite his verbal agreement, Lewis didn't move.

Phillip volunteered, "Give Emily to me. I'll take her to Mrs. Newcomb." He reached for the child.

Emily squirmed, but Phillip's experience with children prompted him to pop her up to sit on his shoulders with her legs straddling his head. She immediately clutched his hair and laughed gleefully, obviously delighted with her new situation.

Phillip turned to Lillian and said quietly, "You've done enough for one day. Don't bother cooking; we can eat bread and cheese tonight." With Emily on his shoulders, Phillip jogged away across the meadow.

But when the little girl suddenly realized she was being carried away from her parents, she began to kick his chest with her feet and demand loudly between screams, "I want my mama. Put me down. I want my mama. I want my papa!" Her cries escalated until she could be heard across the wagon circle.

Jack shifted Evan in his arms and watched Lillian squint into the darkness, her eyes tracking her husband and the howling child. "Don't worry, Miss Lily Ann; Miss Emily will be fine with Mrs. Newcomb. And that was right thoughtful of the Reverend to suggest a simple meal. At least he appreciates what he has."

CHAPTER SIX

When the train stopped for the night, Phillip's efforts to console the shocked members of the traveling party left him no time to set up their tent. Too weary to manage the set-up alone, Lillian straightened their bedding that was rumpled from her nap with Emily and then laid down to sleep.

But her troubled thoughts refused to be still. Her mind replayed baby Elizabeth's tiny body twitching that final time. She recalled Betsey's eyes, clouded with anger and accusation when she'd tried to tell her that Elizabeth was dead. And then there was Jack's odd statement that at least Phillip appreciated what he had—maybe she'd misjudged him; she'd thought Jack didn't like Phillip. Nevertheless, his liking Phillip didn't change a thing: Jack was still a heathen.

She shivered, missing her quilt. The tremors reminded her of the sparks that had shot along her nerves when Betsey finally realized that baby Elizabeth was dead. It had taken Lewis more than an hour to calm Betsey, and her friend's hysterical cries still echoed hauntingly in her ears.

When Betsey had finally agreed to a funeral for Elizabeth, Phillip performed a hasty graveside service by lantern light. The infant's tiny body, sealed in a wood crate donated by the Newcombs, had been buried beside the trail. Most of the Harmon's Warrensburg friends along with Mr. Scranton and a few other party members had attended the short ceremony.

After the service, while Sally Newcomb tried to comfort Betsey, Lillian had approached Lewis and quietly asked him to please return her quilt. But Lewis had stared blankly at her and then mumbled something about thinking it belonged to Betsey so he'd buried the baby in it.

Lillian had nearly choked on her tongue as she swallowed the rage that rushed to her lips. Her quilt was gone—and there was no way to get it back!

She rolled over and stared into the darkness.

And then there was that Vargas woman. Why she'd come to the baby's funeral, Lillian couldn't figure out; it wasn't as if Desiree was a friend of the Harmons—or their baby. But she'd stayed after the service—visiting with the men, Lillian recalled with a sharp stab of resentment.

Jack had been there, too. He'd chosen the gravesite. And Tom Newcomb had helped him dig the hole. After the service, while everyone else stood around talking in the lantern light, Jack and Tom had filled in the grave and pounded a wood cross in the ground to mark it. They'd ended the brief service by piling rocks around the cross to secure it.

And when Desiree had cornered Phillip, Lillian felt Jack's eyes on her. Well, she was proud of herself for not acting on her feelings—she'd have liked nothing better than to pull that woman's hair out. But she knew God would never approve of such vengeful behavior. And Jack had been watching. So she'd forced a smile and told Phillip she was tired and would leave him to visit. Phillip, in the middle of a theological explanation of where infants go when they die, merely nodded and resumed talking.

Jack had fallen into step beside her and accompanied her through the darkness to her wagon. It was a thoughtful and gentlemanly thing to do. She wished it had been Phillip. But Phillip was too busy winning the world.

Oh, God, forgive me! I shouldn't think such horrible thoughts. Phillip is secure in my love—that's why he feels free to reach out to other people—and that's why we are here. What is wrong with me to have such jealous, evil thoughts?

She shifted onto her back and studied the canvas bonnet overhead.

Where is Phillip? It's getting late. Surely he isn't still talking to Miss Vargas.

Her thoughts reverted to Jack. "Are you all right, Miss Lily Ann?" he had inquired when they'd reached her wagon. She knew he hadn't been asking if her arms and legs and eyes and ears were in good working order. He knew she'd been a faithful friend to Betsey. That she'd been there to pry Evan loose when his foot got stuck. And when Emily became hysterical. And when Elizabeth died. And when Emily and the dead baby needed a place to ride. And when someone had to tell

Betsey about her baby's death.

Oh, yes, Jack was sensitive—even if he was a heathen.

Lillian sat up. She drew her knees to her chest and wished she could wrap up in her quilt. But it was gone.

In a hole.

Covered with dirt.

Wrapped around a dead baby.

Her self-control cracked. She began to sob—so loudly she didn't hear Phillip climb into the wagon.

"Sweet Lillian, I'm sorry I was gone so long. You deserve to cry." He gathered her into his arms and held her tight to his heart.

She buried her face in his neck, breathing in his familiar sage scent.

"What a day you've had."

Safe in her husband's embrace, Lillian wept out her sorrow. At last, comforted by his gentleness and tender endearments, she fell asleep.

Morning found them both bleary-eyed and stiff. Phillip went to care for the oxen while Lillian built up the fire and prepared a pot of coffee. She couldn't help noticing that there was no fire beside the Harmon wagon and no sign of Betsey. Phillip returned just as she poured his cup of coffee.

As Phillip reached for the hot beverage, Lewis climbed out the back of his wagon. Phillip looked up. "Good morning, Lewis. How about a cup of coffee?"

Lewis walked over and took it, offering Lillian a grateful nod.

She had to force herself to hand him the cup of hot liquid instead of throwing it at him because all she could think about was that he had robbed her of her quilt. She turned quickly away and busied her hands with cooking breakfast.

The wagons began rolling shortly after the sun crested the horizon from behind the distant purple mountains. Lillian spent the morning lying on the blankets on the floor of the wagon, wretchedly wondering if the prayers of the ladies in the missionary society would do her any good now that she no longer had the quilt. Desperate for peace, she closed her eyes and tried to imagine that the jolting was the soothing motion of her mother's rocking chair—but the rhythm was far too erratic to be convincing, and she ended up feeling restless and irritated.

When the train stopped at noon, Lillian slipped away to take care of personal needs. As she returned to the wagon, she saw that Jack Montgomery had stopped to visit with Phillip. She hesitated, considering disappearing out of sight, but Jack spotted her.

"There you are, Miss Lily Ann," he called out; he seemed to delight in using her name at every opportunity, and his soft drawl never failed to unsettle her. "I came by to tell Mr. and Mrs. Harmon that Evan and Emily are both doing fine. They're with Barsina— she's as doting as any mammy—because Mrs. Newcomb is—ah—" he raised his brows, "Mrs. Sanders, the midwife, is with her."

"You will let us know when you have further news,

won't you?" Concern for Sally Mae superseded Lillian's self-consciousness.

"Yes, Miss Lily Ann, I certainly will." Jack nodded to Phillip and lifted his hat to Lillian. Abruptly, he turned on his heel and strode away.

"I've been praying for Jack," Phillip said, earnestly. "He's a good man, he just needs the Lord."

"Yes, I'm sure you're right."

Forgive me, God. I'm afraid I've hardly prayed for Jack. I've been so mixed up with jealousy over Phillip and anger at . . . at. . . ." she stopped her thoughts before they got any further. God would never be pleased that she'd been angry with *Him*! Oh, sometimes being a good Christian was so difficult. No matter how hard she tried, it seemed like she always fell short. God must be terribly disappointed with her. Maybe that's why bad things kept happening.

Well, now was not the time to worry about that. The laundry needed sorting. And they'd eaten their last two slices of bread at noon. When the train began moving, Lillian measured the ingredients for two loaves of bread into the mixing bowl, taking care to hold the bowl steady as the wagon wheels jolted in and out of potholes. With a practiced hand she pinched out the flies that landed on the dough as she stirred it. She spread a clean cloth over the bowl and set it to rise in a secure place.

After giving a good stir to the pot of beans she'd set to soaking yesterday morning, she turned her attention to their dirty clothes, sorting them into two piles—one of colored items and one of whites—to be laundered later.

All the while, the sun beat down. By mid-afternoon the inside of the wagon felt as hot as a blast from the iron cook stove in the kitchen back home when the stoking lid was opened to add more wood. Deciding it would be cooler to walk beside the wagon and that it might in fact relieve some of her frustration, Lillian put on her now-faded bonnet and tied the ribbons under her chin. She pulled on her gloves to protect her hands from the sun and then climbed down and walked beside the wagon.

When they'd left Independence, the grass along the trail had been lush and green, but here, the sun had scorched everything. The tall, dry grass was brittle and sharp-edged and woefully inadequate to nourish the animals. To make matters worse, the metal-rimmed wooden wagon wheels threw up clouds of trail dust that irritated the animals' eyes, noses, and throats, and increased their need for water.

The dust, combined with inevitable perspiration, made Lillian long for a soothing bath in the long copper tub resting on smooth white tiles in a special room in her mother's cool house. She closed her eyes and pictured the former nursery that had been converted into a bathing room . . . the pristine white wallpaper sprinkled with clusters of purple violets, the white lace curtains, and the stained glass window depicting an elegant purple and yellow iris standing tall and serene on its elegant green stem.

She shook herself. There was no use dwelling on that now. Maybe if they camped near a stream tonight she could get a wash-off and do her laundry. The thought perked up her spirits and she meandered along, singing under her breath.

A rabbit bounded across her path. And then a second one, hopping as if his life depended on it—his ears lay flat against his head and his whole body strained forward. When another, fleeing as frantically as the first two, streaked past her, Lillian looked out over the long, dry grass, puzzled to see it waving and swaying as if blown by a strong wind.

Then prairie dogs, more rabbits, and slithering snakes swarmed out of the grass and streamed across the trail. They were joined by a family of fleeing foxes. And scurrying mice, beetles, bugs . . . all of them ignoring the rolling wagons with their deadly wheels.

Flocks of birds appeared out of nowhere and flew overhead, casting moving shadows across the grass. Swarms of flies buzzed around her and moved on in form-shifting black clouds. And prairie chickens, necks outstretched and wings spread, raced madly across the trail.

Bringing up the rear of the train, the cattle began to bellow and bleat. Horses carrying riders or traveling beside the wagons began to snort and whinny and paw the ground. The whole world suddenly shifted with bolting wildlife. Lillian scanned the earth and sky, first puzzled, then alarmed. Where was the predator causing this frenzied migration? In less than five minutes the whole world had erupted in a cacophony of dissonant sound and disorder . . . as if the unseen hand holding everything in place had suddenly let go.

And then she saw them: great black clouds billowing on the horizon. Relieved to think a storm was on its way bringing welcome rain to break the unrelenting heat, Lillian was astonished to hear the wagon drivers' distressed shouts, "Whoa! Whoa!" She looked about in bewilderment; the wagons had never before stopped because of a storm.

The train slowed to a halt. Phillip jumped down from his seat and yelled at her over his shoulder, "Get in the wagon, Lill. There's a prairie fire—about ten miles away—going to find out what to do." He disappeared toward the front of the train.

A prairie fire!

Lillian took another look at the ominous billows looming off to the right and racing closer by the moment. Her mind struggled to comprehend the rising wind shrieking eerily, the flocks of birds screaming overhead, the animals fleeing like a living carpet, the insects swarming in choking clouds, and—she gasped— the now-visible red underbelly of the advancing smoke.

Hoisting herself up the front of the wagon, she perched on the edge of the spring seat and stared at the menacing conflagration. The fire was roaring now—and from this vantage point she could see red flames flaring and twisting in the black clouds headed straight for the wagon train.

Men shouted. Women cried out. Children wailed.

And the animals squealed, squawked, screeched, buzzed.

Her next breath caught the acrid smell of smoke, its pungency instantly stinging her eyes, her nose, her throat. She tried to hold her breath but she gasped for air as terror engulfed her thoughts: We are going to die! We'll be burned alive.

A pair of bent figures suddenly appeared, running parallel to the train—and following them, springing up in a small line—it couldn't be—but it was—flames shot up behind the two men. She squinted. Mr. Scranton and Jack Montgomery—starting *another* fire! Had they gone mad?

Snatching her handkerchief from under her cuff, Lillian covered her nose and stared through smarting eyes at the black billows laced with red, orange, and yellow flames. Writhing in terrible black smoke, casting an eerie, luminous, dancing light over everything, the approaching wildfire picked up speed as it rushed toward them.

Drawn by the magnitude and sheer power of the terrifying sight, Lillian couldn't pull her eyes away. Then, while she watched, mesmerized, that little strip of fire inched away from the train. It crawled, ever-so-slowly, against the wind. Suddenly, in a long, loud whoosh, the low line of fire was sucked toward the inferno's racing fury. The two fires collided in a crescendo of crackling, screaming wind that climaxed in a deafening shriek.

Lillian clapped her hands over her ears—but it was too late; her head throbbed and her ears rang as if she'd been hit in the head with her cast iron skillet. In spite of the pain, her spellbound gaze remained fixed on the flames. Astounded, and then in stunned relief, she witnessed the fire shift directions. It roared past the train and raced away across the dry grassland.

In the next moment, Lillian shook herself. The air felt strangely hollow; there was an uncanny silence—a total absence of sound—in stark contrast to the normal continuous hum of the breath and brawn of unharnessed primal energy.

As far as Lillian could see, to where the earth met the sky, the ground sizzled, scorched black as charcoal. Thin smoke plumes twisted up into the air like dangling threads and hot ashes and debris scattered in the wind. Lillian's eyes continued to sting and tear and her nose burned as the acrid smell lingered, unfazed by her wisp of scented linen.

Within a few minutes, Phillip jogged back from the front of the wagon train. Observing that the oxen's eyes were streaming with tears and they were stomping restlessly in their harnesses, he grabbed a rag, dampened it with water, and wiped down their faces. When he'd finished, he filled a bucket with water and offered them each a drink. As he held the bucket, he commented, "That Montgomery is one clever fellow."

"What do you mean?" Lillian replied.

"It was his idea to start a back fire. Honestly, I didn't believe it would work because of the wind, but it was that or certain death." Phillip hooked the bucket on the side of the wagon and climbed up beside Lillian. "I never really thought about it before, but being burned alive is not exactly the way I want to go!"

Lillian shuddered, thinking how close they'd come to such a torturous end.

The wagons began moving, and after an hour of steady driving, the train emerged from the naked, blackened prairie. Lillian climbed down and began to walk; she'd never expected to be glad to see tall grass and prairie dog mounds. But when they passed three crosses marking graves beside the trail, she choked on sadness for her friends. Rebecca had buried her husband, and Betsey—poor Betsey had left her baby behind to be passed by strangers who would never know what a dear child Elizabeth had been. And neither of them would ever be able to bring flowers to the grave and shed their tears of grief.

Lillian swiped at her own tears and raged in her heart, *We didn't die in the fire, but if not that . . . it'll be something else. Where are You, God, in all this suffering?*

Because she wasn't watching where she was going, she stumbled over a large buffalo chip and crashed to the ground. As she picked herself up, she suddenly remembered that there would be no fire tonight or in the morning if she didn't gather "meadow muffins." But she'd neglected to carry her drawstring bag for collecting. Sniffling, she caught up her ruffled apron and dabbed her eyes. Then grasping the apron's two bottom corners, she tied them together to form a pouch and began watching for more chips.

She trudged along, periodically darting off to collect chips and then hurrying back so she wouldn't fall behind. Her gloves and apron would require washing before she could wear them again—and her dress as well, she mused when the heap of chips towered above her waist and reached nearly to her chin.

When they stopped for the evening, she dumped the mountain of buffalo chips into a large prairie dog hole near the front of their wagon, which served as a ready-made fire pit. She looked down at herself and grimaced; between the smoke and the heat, compounded by her fall and the buffalo dung, she was sure she'd never been so dirty in all her life. Oh, how she longed for a bath!

Phillip jumped to the ground beside her. As if he'd heard her thoughts, he gestured toward a copse of trees. "Over there, behind those trees, are some pools of bubbling hot water—Soda Springs, Mr. Scranton called them. This morning he said he hoped we'd reach them by tonight. I didn't say anything to you earlier, not wanting to raise your hopes . . . but in spite of the fire, here we are."

Lillian eyed the trees, resisting the urge to shout a hallelujah.

"What are you thinking?" Phillip questioned with a chuckle a few minutes later when he observed his wife, fists planted on her hips, staring at the mound of buffalo chips.

"That if you weren't too hungry, I could get started on the laundry." She looked up and slanted him a beguiling smile. "If we were to go to those springs right now while everyone else is preparing their food and eating, we just might have some privacy; you could stand guard while I bathe and wash my hair."

Phillip nodded. "I've eaten dust all day on that bench, to say nothing of the smoke, so I'd welcome a dip myself." His blue eyes twinkled at her. "I'll spot for you and you spot for me?"

Her initial response was a slow, wide, roguish smile. "Yes, Sir!" she said. Then she bounded forward and smacked his cheek with an impulsive, enthusiastic kiss.

Phillip slung the two bags of dirty laundry over his shoulder and tucked the scrub board under his arm. Lillian walked beside him, toting a bucket filled with their toiletries and laundry soap, and carrying a change of clean clothes for each of them draped over her shoulder. They held hands as they followed the trail through the trees and then headed downstream to avoid polluting the water for the rest of the party.

When they'd gone a good distance, Phillip indicated a broad, bubbling pool surrounded by green grass and rimmed by shrubs off to the right. Lillian didn't hesitate; she let go of Phillip's hand, dropped the bucket of supplies in the grass, tossed the clothes in a heap beside it, and ran to the water's edge, where she kicked off her shoes.

Phillip followed at a slower pace.

"Hurry up, slow poke!" she teased, looking up from peeling off her stockings.

By the time Phillip had dumped the laundry bags on the grass and propped the scrub board against them, Lillian had stuffed her stockings in the toes of her shoes. Like an excited child, she bent down, hiked up her skirt and petticoat, and eagerly waded into the steaming pool.

Bubbles from the pool's underground spring swelled and popped, gurgled and spurted—and obscured the bottom. So when Lillian accidently stepped in a dip, the lower edges of her garments sloshed in the water. She made a face and then impulsively threw off restraint, surging forward until she was waist deep.

"Ooh, Phillip, it's wonderfully delicious!" She ducked completely under the water, clothes and all, and came up laughing.

Phillip grinned at her, waggled his dark eyebrows, and quickly shucked out of his clothes down to his underpants. Taking a running leap, he joined her in the water. For the next quarter of an hour they bobbed up and down, splashing each other and laughing together like two merry children. The troubles of the past few days were momentarily forgotten, soaked away in the therapy of affection and clean water.

When they were dressed in their dry clothes, Phillip emptied the bags of dirty clothes on the grass beside the pool. While Lillian scrubbed, Phillip rinsed the clean garments and wrung out the water. As she watched her husband, Lillian reflected on her good fortune to have married a man who knew how to pitch in and help with every aspect of life. Even the laundry!

Just as they were finishing, they heard voices approaching the trees that flanked the first pool they'd passed. Turning his head toward the sounds, Phillip squinted through the shrubs. "Look!"

Lillian peered in the direction he indicated in time to see a dozen members of their party making their way to the water. "It's a good thing we came when we did," she observed with a nod.

"And I'm glad I have such a smart wife!" He winked at her.

Lillian grinned back. "Thank you, kind sir!"

By the time they headed to their wagon the temperature was pleasant and daylight had faded into dusk. Lillian threw side glances at Phillip, thinking he looked particularly nice with his black hair slicked back. And his compliment—well, nothing could have more effectively lifted her spirits or enhanced her desire for intimacy.

As they approached the wagon circle, Lillian spotted Betsey leaning against her wagon. Her friend's shoulders sagged and her head drooped forward; dejection weighted every muscle in her body. Lillian plopped her bucket beside her wagon and walked over to her friend.

"Hello, Betsy."

When Betsey did not acknowledge the greeting, Lillian searched her mind for the right words to say, but nothing seemed appropriate. When she'd almost given up, Betsey's vacant gaze came to rest on Lillian.

"Did you hear Elizabeth crying? I-I thought I heard her crying. But then I remembered. She's still sleeping, isn't she?" Betsey's glazed eyes wandered. "But your quilt is keeping her warm . . ."

Lillian averted her face to hide her dismay, and when she finally managed to speak, her whisper was strained. "Yes, Betsey, Elizabeth is still sleeping—in my quilt." Betsey was obviously not living in reality; the trauma had been too much for her.

Lillian leaned against the wagon beside Betsey and waited a few minutes, hoping her presence would help her friend find her way back to reality, but Betsey stared at the ground and didn't speak again.

Lillian finally returned to her own wagon, but anger and helplessness gnawed at her faith. *God, all my life I've believed that You are good. So why did you let baby Elizabeth die? Just look at what it's done to poor Betsey. I don't understand.*

While Lillian made a fire and cooked up a pot of beans, Phillip pounded a tent peg into the ground and strung a rope from the inside rear corner of their wagon to the peg. When the makeshift clothesline was secure, he draped their wet garments over the rope so they would dry overnight.

"Let's sleep on the ground under the wagon," Phillip suggested when he'd hung the last of the clothes. "It's still hot in the wagon, and I don't feel like getting all sticky again, setting up the tent."

"The fresh air would be nice after all the smoke we breathed in today. Besides, the tent smells musty."

Lillian wrinkled her nose. "I think it was still damp along the bottom edges when we folded it up last time."

While Phillip retrieved their bedding and set to work spreading it under the wagon, Lillian retrieved her tortoise shell comb and knelt beside the fire. She bent her head forward, untied the ribbon she used to restrain her hair, and began working through the tangles.

At the sound of approaching footsteps, Lillian turned her head and looked up. Startled to see Jack, she abruptly let go of her hair. It flowed around her shoulders, creating shadows that enhanced the delicate planes of her face and the hollows around her eyes.

Jack removed his hat. "Good evening, Miss Lily Ann."

Lillian quickly swished her hair into her hands, drew it together into one long rope at her nape, and tied it back in a respectable fashion. But she knew by the expression on Jack's face that he'd been watching her.

"I came to report that Mrs. Newcomb has a fine son. Samuel Pierce Newcomb, he is." Why did his warm Southern accent make everything he said sound like music?

Lillian had stayed still while he spoke but now she stood up, determined to overcome her self-consciousness. "And little Emily? Is she doing all right?"

"Totally enthralled with the new baby." Jack grinned, adding, "She's as good a helper as Mrs. Newcomb could wish for."

Emerging from under the wagon, Phillip rose to his feet. "Good evening, Mr. Montgomery."

"Reverend," Jack nodded, acknowledging Phillip's greeting. "I bring news of the Newcomb's new arrival. Mother and son are doing well." He glanced at the flowered bedding under the wagon, shot Lillian a subtle, knowing look, and said to Phillip, "I'd best be going. Have a very pleasant evening." He replaced his hat.

Lillian cheeks flamed with repressed fury and she clenched her hands into fists. *How dare he imply that Phillip and I will be spending intimate time together tonight? Of all the nerve!*

She turned to Phillip with a scathing criticism on her lips, struggling to wait until Jack moved out of earshot.

"Thanks for stopping by. We appreciate the news," Phillip called out his farewell, his gratitude circumventing her outburst.

Jack disappeared into the darkness, whistling softly.

An hour later, Lillian cuddled next to Phillip and listened to his even breathing. She smiled contentedly. After Jack had left their campsite, she'd cautiously voiced her concern over the big man's overt attentiveness, and Phillip had promptly reassured her, "With a wife as lovely as you, I don't blame lonely single men for admiring you—or envying me my good fortune. The Bible says in Proverbs that a virtuous woman is to be prized far above rubies. I've given Mr. Montgomery a lot of thought, and I've concluded that he recognizes your worth."

Lillian snuggled closer to Phillip. Jack's disconcerting ability to rattle her must stem from her own foolish vanity. Tomorrow would be a new day. She would try harder to please God. To be a good wife. After all, she loved Phillip very much and she did so want God to be pleased with her.

CHAPTER SEVEN

As they did every weekday morning, the sentries fired their rifles at six o'clock. Lillian groaned. Oh, how she longed for the day when she could sleep as late as she wished. It really did seem strange; she had never struggled to wake up in the morning . . . not until recently, that is.

As she stared up at the bottom of the wagon, resisting the demands of the day for a few moments, she thought about the morning routine of each family. Everyone hurried about in the early light, kindling a fire, hanging a kettle of water over it, preparing breakfast, milking cows if they had some, breaking down the tents they'd slept in, and finally, repacking their belongings into their wagons. By seven o'clock the wagons were again rolling along the trail.

Although their train had faced some major challenges, nothing matched the constant fear of an Indian attack—being captured was considered a fate far worse than death—and it kept everyone on edge. No Indians had actually been seen, but whoops and shouts echoing in the distance on several occasions had only served to heighten everyone's anxiety and frighten them into constant vigilance.

It had been two weeks since the prairie fire, and

life on the trail had been calm. The sun was well up in the morning sky and the wagons were rolling smoothly along the trail when a shot rang out in the distance. That in itself was not a rare occurrence; the hunters among the party shot wildlife whenever it presented itself. But this shot was followed by a blood-curdling whoop that sent terror gushing through Lillian's veins. It cut off her breath and sent her down flat on her stomach on a crate. Scooting to the side of the wagon, she shifted her head until her right eye lined up with the narrow gap between the oilcloth and the sideboard. She peered out toward the distant hills.

A billowing dust cloud appeared to be tumbling down the dry hillside. Her mouth went dry; not another fire! However, as the cloud drew close, a band of painted, feathered Indians riding bareback on ponies emerged from the cloud and charged ahead of it.

Lillian gasped; those wild creatures were headed directly toward the middle of the wagon train—toward their wagon! The frenzied whoops, the ponies' thudding hoofs, and the swirling dust gave the impression that a whole tribe was involved in the attack.

Shouts and cries went up from the wagons, and Lillian started to shake. But as the riders approached, Lillian blinked and gasped. Her heart, beating double-time, slammed into her ribs. The leader of the attack was wearing a quilt—*her quilt*—wrapped around his shoulders! One brown hand, striped with white lines, clutched two corners of the quilt under his chin, leaving the free ends flapping and snapping behind him.

They've raided Baby Elizabeth's grave!

Rage overcame her fear. Scrambling to the front of the wagon, Lillian balanced on her knees on her hope chest and stuck her head out the front. Phillip's sharp exclamation, "What should I do?" played into her wildly desperate thoughts of somehow heroically rescuing her quilt.

A frantic scream pierced the air, jolting Lillian's already frazzled nerves; she jumped involuntarily and nearly toppled from her perch. As she struggled to right herself without looking down—she didn't want to miss anything—the canvas bonnet covering the Harmon wagon bulged as though someone had fallen against it. Then it shivered in the aftermath of the blow. Abruptly, Betsey burst out the back.

Before Lillian's mind grasped what her friend intended, Betsey leaped to the ground and hurled herself toward the rider flaunting the quilt. Shaking her fists, she shrieked hysterically, "That is Lillian's quilt! Where is my baby? Give me my baby!"

Lillian's breath froze in her throat.

Crazed shouts and whoops rose from the Indians as they rode back and forth along the train, their ponies' feet knocking up the ground and sending puffs of dirt into the air. But the leader of the attack, his face painted with black and white stripes and his head flashing with a full headdress of red-tipped black and white eagle feathers, rode straight at Betsey. He released a corner of Lillian's quilt and sliced it through the air with broad sweeps—as if to chase Betsey away.

Amid the noise and commotion, several more shots were fired.

Betsey screamed and clawed at her chest. She took several weaving steps and then fell to her knees. Lillian tumbled out of the wagon and crashed onto the spring seat beside Phillip as Betsey slumped to the ground.

The quilt, its swirling colors shifting like the images in a kaleidoscope, flew out of the Indian's hand, skimmed through the air whirling like a pinwheel, and scraped across the dry ground. It finally slithered to a stop in a crumpled heap a short distance from Betsey.

Amid high pitched cries and the clattering of hoofs, the noisy raiders departed into the hills and disappeared in a dust cloud.

The wagons ground to a halt. A number of men, Phillip included, jumped to the ground, but long-legged Tomas reached Betsey first. Desiree rushed after him. And tiny Maria, Tomas' wife, trailed behind, fingering her rosary and moaning Ave's.

"Wait! Wait for me," Lewis hollered, leaping to the ground. He dashed toward Betsey, his steps frantic and unsteady; he stumbled over a rock and crashed to his knees. His hat fell off and rolled away in the dirt.

Phillip came alongside him and helped him to his feet. When they reached Betsey, Lewis collapsed on his knees next to her, his big hands fluttering over her bleeding chest in helpless bewilderment. Then he bent over her as though to pick her up—but it quickly became obvious that he couldn't carry her; he was babbling incoherently as he patted her face.

"Let me help," Tomas offered. Without waiting for Lewis's consent, he slid his arms under Betsey's slender frame and lifted her. Phillip helped Lewis get back on his feet and together they followed Tomas.

Her eyes fixed on her friend, Lillian jumped to the ground and started toward the sad little procession— but when Betsey's head lolled sideways and one arm, dripping blood, slid off her chest and dragged lifelessly along the ground, Lillian pressed her hands against the sides of her head as she tried to contain her shock and confusion.

Betsey is dead!

Jack, approaching from his wagon near the end of the train, came up behind Lillian. He saw her wilt, and he caught her as she fainted. He placed her on the ground beside her wagon, then whipped off his hat and began vigorously fanning her face.

Desiree saw Jack catch Lillian. "Did they shoot her too?" she called out, running toward them.

"No, she fainted," Jack growled. In the next breath, he ordered, "Fetch me some water." When she didn't move, he barked at her, "Now!"

By the time Tomas reached the Harmon wagon with Betsey's limp body, several women had joined Jack and Lillian and two ladies from the Warrensburg Oregon Society had collected Emily and Evan and taken them to play with their own children.

When Desiree returned with a tin cup filled with water, Jack took it, barely glancing up and without offering a thank-you. Although Desiree shifted her weight impatiently from one foot to the other, obviously expecting an acknowledgement, Jack ignored her. Completely focused on Lillian, he gently raised her head and held the cup to her lips.

Maria, her beads swinging and praying loudly at the edge of the small knot of people beside the Denbeigh wagon, caught Phillip's attention. His glance moved from Maria to Jack kneeling beside Lillian, her head cradled against the big man's shoulder. Phillip's eyes instantly blazed with anger and he abruptly abandoned Lewis and charged toward them.

A few drops of water slid into Lillian's mouth. Coughing and choking, she regained consciousness. And opened her eyes to find Jack's shoulder behind her head, his warm breath sighing against her cheek, his spicy scent filling her nostrils. She closed her eyes, moaning as she turned her head away from the cup.

At that moment Phillip reached Jack. He grabbed his shoulder and shouted, "What do you think you're doing, Montgomery?"

Lillian's eyes flew open as Desiree clutched Phillip's arm and squeezed, hard. "Calm down! Jack's trying to revive your wife. She fainted when she realized Betsey is dead."

Desiree's stark words snapped Phillip back to reality. "Sorry," he mumbled, stumbling back a step.

"Forget it," Jack replied evenly. He set the cup aside and then slowly withdrew his support from behind Lillian's head. Taking her hand, he pulled her into a sitting position. Grim-faced, Jack got to his feet and motioned for Phillip to take his place beside his wife. With a last glance at Lillian, Jack turned away and joined the men gathered near Betsey's body.

Phillip dropped to his knees beside Lillian. With his hand pressed to her forehead, he studied his wife's pale face. "Are you all right, Lill?"

"Y-yes," she forced the word between her lips; she'd been almost as upset by Jack's close proximity as by Betsy's death. Oh, why couldn't that man just leave her alone?

Phillip straightened and patted her shoulder, nodding and murmuring, "Good, good." His eyes darted to the men standing with Lewis. "Please, stay here and rest, Lill; Lewis needs me." He jumped to his feet and left her to join the men.

Lillian's eyes followed Phillip, but her attention was diverted when Desiree walked over to her quilt that someone had retrieved from the dirt and dumped near Betsey's body. Desiree picked it up and shook it out with several quick snaps and then spread it on the dusty ground, obviously intending to use it as a shroud.

"No! No! No!" Lillian cried out loudly, fiercely, struggling to get up. *Not a second dead body in my quilt!*

Jack heard her desperate protest and swung around in time to see Lillian take a few unsteady but determined steps toward Desiree, her eyes locked on her quilt. Jack dashed toward Desiree. Placating her with a few low words, Jack took possession of the quilt. Then he swung around and met Lillian's frantic gaze with a reassuring nod. In several long strides he reached Lillian and thrust the blanket into her outstretched arms.

Too upset to speak, Lillian hugged her quilt to her heart, unaware that the word **COMFORT**, embroidered in orange floss, cupped her chin. Without a word, Jack rejoined the gathered men, and Lillian returned to her place in the shade of the wagon.

Fear spread like the plague among the members of the wagon train, trapping most of them inside their wagons. Mr. Scranton, recognizing the urgent need to restore order and get the train moving again, assigned Tomas, Phillip, and Tom to immediately dig a grave with their pick axes and shovels—this time in the trail at the front of the wagons where the wheels would roll over the broken ground and remove any trace of activity. This would be one grave the Indians would not desecrate.

Within twenty minutes the men had dug a hole that was over four feet deep. Leaving the dust to settle, the three men shouldered their tools and walked back to the Harmon wagon.

Haste precluded niceties; with palpable fear of another attack hanging heavy in the air, no time was wasted building a casket. Instead, Desiree and Maria wrapped Betsey's body in a sheet that Desiree located in the Harmon wagon.

Still feeling weak and shaken, Lillian watched the proceedings from her place in the shade. When all was ready, Phillip climbed in their wagon to get his Bible, and then he joined Lewis following Tomas and Tom, the self-assigned pall bearers, as they carried Betsey's sheet-encased body toward the gravesite at the front of the train. Loyalty to Phillip and his calling to minister conflicted with her feelings of abandonment.

As an only child, Lillian had often been plagued by loneliness, and now, although she was married, she often still felt alone. Taken up with caring for others, Phillip had forgotten about her. Moisture welled up in her eyes and she crushed her quilt tighter against her chest.

As if reading her mind, Jack came close and squatted down next to her. "Do you wish to pay your respects to Mrs. Harmon?" He offered her his hand.

Lillian suppressed a sad sigh and swallowed hard. She took Jack's hand and let him help her to her feet. Still clutching her quilt, she walked beside Jack to the gravesite, where they joined those who'd gathered to honor Betsey and to support Lewis.

As Tomas and Tom lowered the shrouded body into the freshly-dug hole, Phillip cleared his throat. "We are gathered here to remember the life of Betsey Johnson Harmon, wife of Lewis, mother of Emily, Evan, and Elizabeth, and friend to us all."

The realization that they would be leaving Betsy behind, covered in dirt, in the middle of the trail, to be rolled over by all the wagons heading west, weighed so heavily on Lillian's heart that she didn't hear anything else Phillip said. Tremors shook her body and she bit her lips between her teeth to keep from crying out. When

Jack placed his hand on her back for support, hot tears spilled from her eyes and ran down her face.

"I want to direct your thoughts to the comforting words of John 11:25-26," Phillip said, concluding the brief ceremony. "Jesus said to Mary, 'I am the resurrection and the life. He who believes in Me, though he may die, he shall live. And whoever lives and believes in Me shall never die.' The Betsey we know and love is not dead. Her spirit is alive with God. Forever." He bowed his head, "Shall we pray?"

His prayer was brief; in spite of everyone's sorrow, fear remained the prevailing emotion.

Why, God? Why Betsey? What did she do to deserve to die? Lillian's tormenting questions made her stomach churn.

Phillip took Lewis by the arm and led him away from the grave while Tomas and Tom filled in the hole and smoothed it over.

Along with everyone else, Lillian turned to go back to the wagons. But she had only taken half a dozen steps when the distress in her stomach overpowered her desire to retain her fragile dignity. Dropping her quilt, she rushed toward a nearby bush, where she lost the contents of her stomach.

Despair overwhelmed her; in a mere couple of months her happy little world had become a nightmare of confusion, fear, and death. Oh, how she wished this was all a bad dream and that she would wake up safely snuggled in her own bed in her parents' home

As she straightened up, attempting to clean her

face with the square of flimsy linen she'd snatched from her cuff, Jack was beside her, pushing his large white handkerchief into her hand. While she wiped her mouth, he picked up her quilt and slung it over his shoulder with the bulk of the quilt hanging down his back.

Turning to thank Jack, Lillian was startled to read the word **TRUST** encircled by ivy draped over his shoulder. He offered his arm for her support, but Lillian shook her head and reached for her quilt just as Mr. Scranton passed by.

"Montgomery, join us at the front. Looks like there's a shortcut up ahead. We need to decide if we're going to take it."

"Be right there, Sir." Jack said, passing the quilt to Lillian just as Sally Mae, carrying baby Samuel against her shoulder, approached them.

"Thank you," Lillian said to Jack, clasping her dusty quilt with its message of trust to her heart. "I'll be fine now."

Jack headed toward the men gathered at the front of the train, and Lillian, with Sally Mae beside her, made her way back to her wagon. After saying good-bye to Sally Mae, she climbed inside the wagon.

Alone in the dark cavern, Lillian sank down on a crate to wait for Phillip's return. Her stomach continued to churn, and she felt weepy and forsaken, burdened with questions she couldn't answer.

A few minutes later she heard Phillip's voice in the distance. Her heart lifted; she still had Phillip.

Impulsively, she leaned over her hope chest to look out the front. But consternation followed her relief. Phillip was not alone—he was engaged in an intense conversation with Desiree.

A surge of jealousy overshadowed her shock and sorrow when she noticed that Desiree was again wearing her low-cut white blouse. To make matters worse, one sleeve had slipped from her shoulder to rest just above her elbow, offering a prime view of her ample bosom to anyone who happened to glance her way.

Lillian closed her eyes as compounded misery washed over her soul.

CHAPTER EIGHT

The wind blew buffalo chip smoke into Lillian's face. She gagged, suddenly feeling cold and clammy and nauseous. Pressing her hands to her mouth, she swallowed hard, determined not to retch. But she couldn't help wondering what was wrong with her; she'd been cooking over buffalo chips every day for more than a month, and the residual smoke had never bothered her before today.

She closed her eyes and tried to refocus.

Suddenly, the breath was sucked out of her body as a blast of force slammed into her. She felt her feet leave the ground. In the next instant, she smacked into the dirt. Something struck her legs, beating at her repeatedly. She opened her mouth to scream but could only gasp and cower.

When she finally opened her eyes, Jack Montgomery's brawny figure loomed over her, slapping out flames in the skirt of her gown with his hat. She groaned; she'd always taken care to stand upwind from her fire, but today she hadn't even thought about it.

Jack sank back on his haunches. His dark eyes burned in his pinched face and his voice grated, hoarse with anxiety. "You must be more careful, Miss Lily Ann. You could have been seriously burned."

Lillian grimaced and sat up. As she rubbed the bruised spot on her left elbow caused by her harsh landing, she burst into tears. Furious at herself for another embarrassing display of unsteady emotions in front of Jack, she hurriedly brushed away the misty signs of her weakness. But when a convulsive eruption sent her into dry heaves, she groaned and sank down on her good elbow. The tears surged again—and this time she couldn't control them. Oh, what was wrong with her?

Tossing his hat aside, Jack rolled forward to his knees. His fingers grasped Lillian's shoulder in a reassuring gesture as leaned toward her and inquired solicitously. "Sorry I knocked you down, Miss Lily Ann. Are you hurt?"

Phillip, in a discussion with Desiree only a dozen yards away, glanced toward the commotion. When his gaze narrowed on Jack on his knees bent over Lillian, Phillip deserted his conversation mid-sentence and ran at Jack, snarling, "I've had about enough of you, Jack Montgomery. Keep your hands off my wife!" Lunging at Jack as he rose to his feet, Phillip delivered a rough shove.

Jack's sturdy frame absorbed the attack and he held his ground. But Phillip, slighter in stature, lost his balance, lurched sideways, and crashed in the dirt.

Jack picked up his hat, turned his back on Phillip, and said softly, "Take care of yourself and Junior, Miss Lily Ann." He settled his hat on his head and walked away without a backward glance.

"I can't turn my back for a minute but what that fellow is fawning over you," Phillip shouted, scrambling to his feet and rushing to her.

Lillian began to sob.

"Mind, I'm not blaming you," Phillip defended himself, "but would you mind telling me what Jack did to you—why are you on the ground?"

Not blaming her! Only God knew how hard she'd tried to discourage Jack's attentiveness, sometimes to the point of being downright rude.

Smoke from their fire swirled around them, sending Lillian into another spasm of dry heaves. Tight-lipped and silent, Phillip picked her up and moved her closer to their wagon, away from the smoke.

Lillian's queasiness gradually subsided. "My . . . my skirt," she sniffed, holding out her gown to display the charred edges surrounding a gaping hole that exposed her singed petticoat.

Shock replaced Phillip's belligerence. His voice dropped to an appalled whisper. "I didn't see . . . how did that happen?"

"I-I was bending over the fire." She caught a ragged breath. "I wasn't feeling well—so I closed my eyes. The next thing I knew, someone threw me to the ground and began hitting my legs. When I opened my eyes, Mr. Montgomery was beating out the flames in my skirt with his hat." She eyed him reproachfully. "He saved me from a very bad accident."

Scowling, Phillip grumbled ungraciously, "I suppose I owe him an apology." But in the next breath he justified his attitude, "It's just that he always seems to be Johnny-on-the-spot where you're concerned, and that makes me furious. You're *my* wife."

"Nobody doubts that, Phillip," she reassured softly. "Especially not now—" she lifted shy eyes, "with Junior on the way."

"Junior?" He repeated the word as if searching his mind to identify its meaning. Then his face softened and elation filled his blue eyes. "You mean you're . . ?"

"Yes, Phillip." She smiled up at him. "That's why I've been so qualmish and emotional these last few weeks."

She didn't tell him she hadn't realized her condition until Jack identified it; telling Phillip that the observation had come from Jack would only create further tension between the two men, and right now she'd had about all of that she could take. She had other things to think about.

Like a coming baby!

* * *

After the sun went down, Phillip rebuilt their fire. In the cool of the evening they sat on the grass, leaning against the right front wagon wheel. Lillian's freshly washed and dried-on-the-line quilt covered their laps with the words COMFORT, PATIENCE, and HOPE facing up at them. Lillian curved into the shelter of her husband's arm, and their voices murmured in low whispers.

"I've been thinking," Phillip offered pensively, "maybe we should go to California instead of Oregon. The need for Christian workers is much greater there, particularly among the miners."

Not really worried that he might be serious, Lillian asked, "How soon do we have to decide?"

"We have about a week. Mr. Larson, one of our scouts, thinks we'll crest the steepest section of the Rockies in the next day or two; then a few more days and we'll reach the trail that heads south to California." Phillip stared into the dancing flames as he mused out loud, "The Newcombs are going to Oregon—and Lewis, too, along with the rest of the Warrensburg families. But Tomas and a few others intend to go to California. Tomas thinks he and his family, being Spaniards, will have an easier time fitting into the culture in California, as opposed to Oregon."

Lillian frowned and questioned naively, "Why would that be?"

"Well, not many settlers moving to Oregon are of Spanish descent, whereas California already has a large Spanish-speaking population."

"I see," Lillian nodded then added, "With our prospective family in mind, I'll admit I lean toward Oregon."

CHAPTER NINE

The Scranton party headed into the upper Rockies. By easy grades the trail wound up almost eight thousand feet to the summit of South Pass.

Illness had struck the wagon train members, and nearly a dozen folk had succumbed. Although some thought it was from drinking bad water, most of the party believed it was the result of getting too hot in the daytime and then chilled at night. Whatever the cause, it made strong men struggle to care for their animals and little children cry inconsolably. But worst of all, when a mother fell ill she had a difficult time keeping an eye on her children.

Lillian wept when she heard that the Cooper's four-year-old daughter Leticia had tried to jump to the ground from the tongue of their wagon, but she'd slipped and been run over by three wagons before the train managed to stop. And then there was little Bobby Hoyt; while the oilcloth bonnet on the Hoyt wagon was pushed up to let fresh air move through, he grabbed a shrub that brushed the side of the wagon—and he didn't let go. He'd been jerked out of the wagon and plunged down a sharp cliff to his death.

Lillian thanked God every day that they would be in Oregon before she gave birth. And she stubbornly refused to entertain the prospect of California as their destination even though Phillip had mentioned it several more times and twice she'd heard him discussing it with Tomas—the second time, she'd heard a woman's voice in the conversation, and although they'd been too far away to be certain, she suspected the woman was Desiree.

After another tiresome meal of beans and cornbread—her recipe box offering meal options remained in her trunk; now that Betsy was gone she had no heart to get it out—Lillian brought up the subject of their destination.

Phillip replied rather sharply, "I still haven't made up my mind, Lillian, so you can stop asking me about it. I'll decide when the time comes. And I expect you to trust me, whatever I decide. Right now, I have other things to think about."

He paused and rubbed his forehead, staring at the ground as he confided, "Tom Newcomb is pretty sick. And there's been talk that if he isn't better tomorrow, we may have to leave them behind. The incline has been relatively easy so far, but tomorrow we should reach the crest and begin heading down. And that's much harder than going up, you know."

Shock that anyone would consider leaving the Newcomb's behind filled Lillian with fear . . . and from that point she kept quiet; there was no need to trouble Phillip further when he was already concerned for his friend. But both topics dominated her prayers. *Oh, Lord, please help Tom Newcomb get well. And please,*

please—I don't want to go to California. I want to go to Oregon.

The next afternoon, after the entire train had successfully crossed the highest point of South Pass, the wagons inched along. One at a time, with wheels locked and the front wheels repeatedly blocked with rocks to prevent the wagons from over-running the oxen, the wagons jerked and squeaked their way down the steep grade.

A short distance along the downward trail, the path made a particularly sharp bend. Everyone waited as each wagon took its turn maneuvering the treacherous section of the trail. Lillian sat on the spring seat beside Phillip and watched Lewis Harmon's wagon make the curve, watched the loose rocks and gravel thrown up by his wheels fly off the edge of the cliff.

When it had safely rounded the bend, it was their turn. Lillian climbed down and walked a safe distance behind the wagon. After Phillip had slowly and carefully guided their wagon around the curve, Lillian walked over to the cliff edge and looked down. She shuddered at the sight: broken wagon parts lay strewn over the ground below.

As each wagon took its turn, she held her breath, praying it would make its way to safety. When the Newcomb wagon, sixth after the Denbeigh's, approached the curve, Lillian remembered what Phillip had said about Tom Newcomb being ill. Unconsciously, she held her breath.

Rear wagon wheels measured fifty inches in

diameter but front wheels were a bit smaller, only forty-four inches—designed for just such challenging turns. But as attested to by those wagons smashed to bits at the bottom of the cliff, there were no guarantees.

As the rear of the Newcomb wagon swung around, the back outside wheel popped out of the rut. The rear axle snapped with a loud crunch. The wagon slumped and swerved in the loose gravel. Tom cracked his whip down hard on his double yoke of oxen in an effort to jerk the wagon out of its slide. But nothing was sufficient to stop the pull of gravity. The wagon skidded. Then it picked up momentum, pulling the oxen with it over the edge. Tom's shout became an echo.

And then, while Lillian watched in horror, Sally Mae, clutching baby Samuel to her chest with little Emily Harmon clinging to her skirt, ran up to the cliff edge. The Newcomb wagon sailed through the air and smashed below in a cloud of dust and grain and dry goods that billowed up around the splintered wagon. It was a shocking sight. The oxen were nothing more than brown splats—and Tom was nowhere to be seen. Oh, poor Sally Mae!

God, where are you? Don't you care about Sally Mae and her baby? And what about Tom? How could you do this to Tom?

The continual sickness and death—not just of the members of their own party, but of the parties that had gone before and left evidence of their hardships behind: grave markers, rotting animal carcasses and bleached bones, furniture, dishes, crates of belongings—further hardened Lillian's heart. God obviously didn't care.

As she struggled with her grief and despair, she realized Phillip had continued driving their wagon down the trail. He could not have seen the Newcomb's wagon go over the edge or he surely would have stopped. She looked back one final time. The tragic picture of Sally Mae standing on the precipice was seared into her mind. How could she ever forget it?

The train covered only three miles that day. Lillian felt sick at heart and too weary to stir herself to do more than serve Phillip cold beans and dry cornbread for dinner. Not a good meal for a man who'd worked hard all day, but the day's tragedy had sucked all motivation out of her.

Sensing her wretchedness, Phillip ate without comment. And later, after a simple service in memory of Tom Newcomb, he merely suggested she get some sleep.

Returning to their wagon alone, too exhausted to prepare a makeshift bedroom below the wagon, Lillian unrolled their bedding between the crates in their wagon. She changed into her night clothes, wrapped her quilt around her weary body, and lay down on the floor.

A few minutes later Phillip stuck his head between the back flaps. "Mr. Scranton has called a meeting of the men," he informed her. "I'll be back shortly."

Lillian sighed heavily and closed her eyes.

But sleep would not come.

All she could see every time she closed her eyes

was a stricken Sally Mae staring down at her smashed dreams. Lillian finally dozed off, but even in a half sleeping state she worried about what would become of Sally Mae and her little Samuel.

She moaned so loudly she woke herself up. Her nightdress was drenched with perspiration and twisted so tightly around her waist that she could hardly move. She pushed back her hair and wiped the dampness from her forehead and then flipped the quilt to one side. As she tugged at her nightdress, finally freeing herself sufficiently to sit up, she thought it seemed unusually dark outside—clouds must have covered the moon.

And she was alone.

Where was Phillip?

Lillian hated being left alone. Even though she'd told Phillip that she felt abandoned when left alone, he had a hard time understanding, much less sympathizing. Coming from a large family, he reveled in solitude and often left her alone without giving her feelings serious consideration. And it wasn't as if she didn't share his enthusiasm for the gospel, but she had to admit that the reality of the demands of ministry was far different than her idealistic fantasy.

Lillian fell back with a sigh and pulled her quilt back over her legs. Staring into the darkness, she wished she could sleep forever, to forget her heartache in blessed oblivion.

Lantern lights flickered, spreading bobbing shadows on the oilcloth bonnet above her as they came close. Indistinct female voices mingling with men's lower tones came from the direction of the Harmon wagon. Lillian wondered what was taking place but she didn't have sufficient motivation to move. But when she heard Jack Montgomery's soft drawl, curiosity got the better of her. She rolled to her knees and crawled to the front of the wagon.

Leaning over her hope chest, Lillian peeked out. And wondered why Sally Mae Newcomb was standing at the back of the Harmon wagon. Along with Lewis. And Jack, Phillip, Tomas—and Maria and Desiree! She watched Sally Mae climb into Lewis's wagon. Saw Lewis hand Emily up to Sally Mae. She heard a baby cry and realized it was Samuel.

So, Sally Mae was going to stay in her friend's wagon. That was an obvious solution, she concluded. After all, Sally Mae had no provisions—nothing, whereas Lewis had plenty of supplies but no wife. And no one to take care of his children.

She saw Sally Mae hand down several blankets and a feather pillow to Lewis, who turned away, his shoulders sagging as he dumped the bedding on the ground beside his wagon. As if to shut out the world, Sally Mae tugged on the canvas edges at the back of the Harmon wagon. But not before Lillian saw the glisten of tears on her cheeks.

Grief mixed with homesickness sucked Lillian into a vortex of despair. *Oh, I wish we'd never left home! God, where are You? I was taught that you care—but that was a lie.*

CHAPTER TEN

When the wagons stopped for lunch the next day, Lillian jumped to the ground and lifted her face to the breeze, breathing in the aroma of growing things. She smoothed her hands over her slightly mounded belly and found herself smiling with renewed optimism. But when Phillip jumped down beside her with his Bible clutched in his hands, she broke out in a cold sweat.

"Phillip," she gasped, "who-who died?" She pressed her hand over her heart to calm her burst of panic.

"What?" Phillip stopped, eyeing her with a puzzled expression. "Nobody died. Why?"

"I-I just wondered; you don't usually—read your Bible at lunch." She gestured toward the leather-bound book he held.

His short laugh held no humor. "Not a funeral—a wedding."

"A wedding!" Lillian couldn't disguise her astonishment. "Whose wedding?"

"Lewis and Sally Mae." He shrugged. "I told them they couldn't share the same wagon without getting married; it wouldn't be right."

"Oh." Lillian turned away. What a cold, matter-of-fact way to deal with life's tender side. But why should she be surprised? Since they'd set out on this journey, nothing seemed to be quite as she had believed it ought to be. Necessity forced people to do a lot of things they would otherwise never consider. Like bury your baby by the side of the road. Or marry your best friend's husband.

Her glance swept the green hillside dotted with a profusion of wild orange poppies. Flowers. Flowers for a bride!

On impulse, she turned and headed up the hillside, picking the cheerful-headed blooms as she went. Halfway up the hill, her hands filled with a generous bouquet, Lillian stopped, straightened up, and swung around to look back toward the wagons.

The purple Rocky Mountains in all their majestic ruggedness towered off to the left, forming an awe-inspiring backdrop to her insignificance. On the right, rolling hills strewn with wildflowers eased into a lush basin that extended as far as she could see. The beauty of the wilderness and the vastness of creation inspired renewed faith in her heart. She skipped down the hillside toward Sally Mae, who stood near the back of the Harmon wagon, surrounded by her friends from the Warrensburg Oregon Society.

"Excuse me." Lillian pushed through the circle of women and thrust the simple bouquet into Sally Mae's hands. "I picked these for you—to make the day special," she whispered shyly.

Sally Mae gave Lillian a weak smile. "What a thoughtful thing to do. Thank you, Lillian." Moisture welled in Sally Mae's eyes; her thin face looked strained and it was obvious she was struggling to be brave.

Lillian's eyes smarted and it took all her courage to smile back.

When Lewis's oxen lowed loudly, Lillian, glad for a diversion, backed out of the group and turned to look for Phillip among the men clustered near the front of the Harmon wagon.

And met Jack's gaze.

He inclined his head toward Sally Mae and gestured toward her poppy bouquet, raising his brows and nodding his approval.

Lillian felt her face flush and she immediately looked away. But after a moment, she glanced back at him. When she saw that he was still watching her, she abruptly rejoined the women.

Noting the interchange between Jack and Lillian, Desiree's eyes narrowed and her lips flattened into a straight line. She tossed back her long hair and headed straight for Jack.

* * *

"I didn't think to bring along any clothing to accommodate a pregnancy," Lillian confided to Sally Mae one evening about a week after the wedding.

"I'd give you mine but they were all lost . . ." Sally Mae's eyes clouded and she averted her face. After a moment she regained her composure and turned back, suggesting, "I'll look through Betsey's things. She was slightly larger than you, so maybe some of her regular garments would solve your problem. At least temporarily."

In addition to several dresses, Sally Mae found a generous length of flowered calico in robin's-egg blue— enough to make a long-sleeved, full-skirted empire waist dress. While Lillian was not a seasoned seamstress, she had produced her first needlepoint sampler when she was eight years old, so she embarked on her new project with more determination than confidence.

She worked tirelessly for three days, first cutting and then stitching together the fabric pieces. She added a ruffle around each wrist and a deep flounce at the hem. There was even enough material left over to refurbish her disgracefully faded blue bonnet.

Chewing on her lower lip, Lillian viciously stabbed the needle in and out of the fabric as she hemmed the skirt of her new dress. This morning Phillip had told her he'd made a final decision: They would go to California. When she'd started to question him, he'd stopped her, said his mind was made up. She'd bit her tongue then, determined not to disgrace herself with an angry outburst . . . like some of the shrewish wives in their party who embarrassed themselves by arguing loudly with their strong-minded husbands.

Finally, in the late afternoon she finished the last stitch and tied the final knot. "And just in time, too!" she voiced her satisfaction, remembering Phillip had mentioned they would arrive at Fort Hall before dark.

* * *

It had been three months since the Scranton party's wagons rolled away from Independence, Missouri; it had taken a month longer than anticipated to reach Fort Hall. Supplies were low and tempers were short. Rude as civilization was in the outpost, a couple of days—and nights—free from anxiety over the unknown dangers lurking along the trail were welcome indeed. The weary band would regroup, restock, and arrange for repairs. And a few of the men would have a drink—or two.

Phillip was already up and gone when Lillian awoke. She stretched and slowly scooted into a sitting position. Her new gown, draped over the crate of hymnals, caught her eye. Energized by the hope that feeling attractive and civilized would lift her spirits, she discarded her nightgown and donned the dress.

Smoothing the flowered garment over her rounded abdomen, she reminded herself that her dearest hope was soon to become a reality; she and Phillip were going to have a baby. So perhaps she could forgive Phillip for disregarding her objections and deciding they were going to California. After all, God had granted her heart's chief desire, and He would not want her to be an ill-tempered wife.

Lillian hummed under her breath as she climbed out of the wagon. She shook out the wrinkles in her gown and felt a surge of excitement as, just for an instant, she imagined she was looking out the parlor window in her parents' home, waiting for Phillip to come courting—he in his pressed black suit, polished boots, and stiffly-starched white shirt; she in a new gown in the latest fashion. A smile turned up the corners of her mouth as she smoothed her chestnut hair and re-tied the ribbons on her refurbished bonnet. Phillip had been captivated by her delicate beauty—and she'd been captivated by his twinkling eyes and quirky smile . . . and impressed and inspired by his intense desire to go west and preach the gospel. She loved Phillip so much—and now they were going to have a baby!

"You look as pretty as a cornflower," Phillip exclaimed, interrupting her reflection as he came around the side of the wagon. His sweet words further eased the sting of her disappointment over their destination and the impending separation from Sally Mae.

A short while later, Phillip reined their wagon to a halt in front of the log post structure with a sign over the door in bold black letters: HUDSON'S BAY COMPANY.

"Wait here, Lill. I'll be right back." He flung the words over his shoulder as he hopped to the ground and headed toward the front door to collect the purchases he'd ordered earlier that morning.

After sitting on the spring seat in the merciless heat for ten minutes, Lillian's discomfort got the better of her. Intent on finding Phillip, she climbed down, shook out her skirt, and headed up the wooden walk.

Although she vaguely heard the mercantile door open and then bang shut, her eyes were focused on her feet as she bemoaned the worn state of her best shoes. A soft whistle made her look up—straight into the brown eyes of none other than Jack Montgomery.

"Well, aren't you a vision of loveliness, Miss Lily Ann," Jack drawled, lifting his hat to her. There was no missing the warm admiration in his eyes or the flattery in his words.

Determined to let nothing divert her from her good spirits, not even Jack and his disturbing attentiveness, she bobbed a slight curtsey, mustered a "Good morning, Sir," and slipped past him in a flurry of flowered skirt and petticoat.

But she couldn't make herself completely ignore the handsome Southerner; when she got to the door she impulsively ducked her head to steal a backward glance around the side of her bonnet . . . just in time to see Desiree approach him.

Transfixed, Lillian watched the sultry woman raise one hand in a slow, provocative motion and languorously run her fingers through her curling dark hair. Eying the big man through half-closed, black-fringed eyes, Desiree purred in her sultry voice, "Ah, Jack. Just the man I wished to see. I need your expert advice . . ." Slipping her hand in the crook of Jack's arm, she brazenly lifted her face to smile seductively at him.

Lillian's lips tightened in disgust as she reached for the door.

Unexpectedly, it opened in her face.

"Lillian!" Smiling his crooked smile, Phillip grasped her arm and swung her around toward their wagon. "Sorry it took me so long, my pretty cornflower."

Lillian's eyes collided with Jack's; he was watching her from the street. And suddenly, unbidden, her mind replayed his words from the night she'd twisted her ankle: *"How did a passionate little thing like you get hooked up with such a do-gooder?"*

Cross with herself for remembering his boldly inappropriate comment, Lillian turned to Phillip. Coquettishly batting her eyelashes and in her best imitation of Desiree's sultry cooing, she purred, "Ah, Phillip. You're just the man I wished to see." She forced herself to gaze steadfastly into her husband's darkening blue eyes.

Phillip chuckled, obviously charmed by his wife's attempt to flirt with him.

Lillian held her head high and refused to look at Jack; she would not give that bothersome man such satisfaction.

CHAPTER ELEVEN

The evening before the train reached the fork in the trail where the Snake River followed the Raft River toward California, many of Phillip and Lillian's friends, including Lewis and Sally Mae, came by for a final goodbye. Lillian and Sally Mae squeezed each other's hands and cried. As she gave Sally Mae a parting hug, Lillian whispered, "Godspeed, my friend."

In the morning, the wagons bound for Oregon pulled out first. While Phillip and Lillian watched from their spring seat, Phillip gleefully informed Lillian that there were only nine wagons going to California. When she asked him why he was so pleased, he replied, "A small train will make better time and that will greatly improve our chances of arriving in Sacramento by September—before the weather turns cold." He turned to her with a smile, "And that will be good for you—and for Junior, too."

Lillian made a mental review of the wagons that would take the left fork with them. Jack Montgomery, with two wagons, was now the lead man. Behind him, also with two wagons, came the Sanfords—George and Bella and their five children. Phillip and Lillian came next. Tomas and Maria Velasquez and Desiree Vargas, all in one wagon, followed the Denbeighs. Rebecca

Lawson and little Milton rode in her wagon, which was now being driven by Isaac Prewitt, a widower with three teen-age sons. Mr. Prewitt had taken an interest in Rebecca and her baby following Martin's death, and they had announced that they would be getting married when they reached Sacramento. Mr. Prewitt's two wagons, driven by the older two of his three sons, brought up the rear.

When the train stopped for the night in a narrow, grassy meadow bordered on both sides by a thicket of trees, Jack directed the wagons to park in two parallel rows instead of the more conventional circle. The cattle were tethered on long ropes at the far end, where lush grass promised them good grazing.

While the men met to determine a plan for patrol duty, Lillian walked across the aisle between the wagons to introduce herself to Mrs. Sanford; up to this point they had only nodded and greeted each other from a distance because the Sanford wagon had been eighteen wagons behind the Denbeigh wagon in the former rotation.

Short and plump, Bella Sandford was the jolly mother of five children ranging in age from three to seventeen, and Lillian had envied the bustling and laughter that took place each evening around their fire.

After a brief visit with Mrs. Sandford, Lillian returned to her own wagon. She built a fire, cooked a pot of rice and beans, and then baked the bread she'd set to rise earlier in the day. Briefly, she wished for some fresh meat—maybe tomorrow Phillip would shoot another bird or a squirrel. To her surprise and his credit, Phillip had proved fairly handy with his gun, and they'd enjoyed a few roasted birds, a squirrel once, and at least a dozen rabbits.

As she stowed things back in the wagon after their evening meal, Phillip retrieved his Bible. "I'll try not to be gone long, Lill," he said, "but don't wait up for me. Mr. Prewitt and I are going to discuss the Scriptures." He gave her a quick peck on the cheek before disappearing into the darkness.

Lillian spread their bedding under the wagon; it was far too warm to sleep inside their musty tent—or in the wagon, for that matter. Four sheets and two tablecloths draped around the wagon's bottom edges provided privacy, and they had become quite accustomed to sleeping in their makeshift bedroom.

A couple of hours later, Lillian shifted uncomfortably and woke enough to realize that yes, Nature was definitely calling. She looked over at Phillip, who was snoring softly, and decided there was no way she could wait until morning.

Careful of her protruding belly, she scooted under the closest edge of the screening sheet and found herself in the grass on the tree-side of their wagon. She sat up and looked around. The wagon bonnets looked ghostly in the shadows cast by the sliver of a moon's dim light, but the familiar sounds of softly lowing cattle made her feel secure. A thick clump of shrubs a short distance away from the wagon had provided her with privacy earlier that evening, so she quickly made her way toward their dark shadows.

When she'd returned to the wagon, she stopped for a moment to stare up at the stars. Her thoughts drifted to her parents back home. Always a doting, indulgent presence in her life, Lillian's father, Austin Cartwright, an architect, was the only son of the wealthy former Governor and Mrs. Sterling Cartwright. And her mother, Eleanor Carson Cartwright, although descended from humbler means and ten years younger than Austin, had fascinated him the first time he saw her because she reminded him of "Beautiful Betty," an oil painting by Andrew Lynch, a fellow student at the École des Beaux-Arts in Paris, where he'd studied as a young man.

The Cartwrights had raised Lillian, a miracle baby after ten barren years of marriage, in a manner befitting their status, pampering and protecting her from the harshness of reality and delighting in her delicate beauty that was a reflection of her exquisite mother.

When the handsome young lawyer, James Sinclair, opened a practice in their community and began attending St. Matthew's Presbyterian, he quickly settled his attentions on the lovely Lillian. She'd been flattered—and her parents had been ecstatic. That is, until the zealous theology student, Phillip Denbeigh, had won the bid on her Christmas basket.

When it became obvious that the mission-minded Phillip had captured the pampered Lillian's imagination, Eleanor Cartwright lamented to her husband that he would never have had a chance with her if the eminently suitable James hadn't been home sick with a bad cold on the night of the Christmas social.

Lillian gazed up at the pin-prick stars in the black night sky and acknowledged that she'd been as equally unprepared for Phillip's dedication to ministry that often took precedence over her expectations as she was for the grimness of tragedy and death that her parents had purposely excluded from her perfect little world.

Twinges of sadness and regret scraped at the edges of her mind. She would never see her parents again. Never feel their care. Never be the adored object of their devotion. She ran her fingers over the burn on her hand . . . never again live a life of ease and luxury.

While she stood there, musing, she heard the soft murmur of voices a couple of wagon lengths away. Impulsively, she took a step toward the sounds, squinting to see who was speaking.

The tall figure standing under the oak tree was Jack Montgomery—she would know him anywhere. And there was no mistaking the person approaching him was Desiree Vargas. While Lillian watched, Desiree moved close to Jack, tipped up her head, shook out her long hair, and raised her arms to encircle Jack's neck.

Lillian gasped out loud.

Jack's head turned abruptly toward her. Even as his hands grasped Desiree's arms, the sultry woman cooed in her throaty voice, "Yes, *carino*, you may kiss me." Rising on tip-toes, she pressed a swift kiss to Jack's mouth.

Mortified, Lillian dropped to the ground and

crawled under her wagon. Hidden from everyone and everything, she covered her hot cheeks with her palms and stared up in the darkness at the wagon's confining underbelly.

Her thoughts ran around and around. She felt like a rat caught in a maze. *Oh, how could I have been so gauche, gasping and gaping like a schoolgirl? How on earth will I face them tomorrow?*

Sleep would not come. Over and over, she replayed the scene in her mind. And every time her memory came to the kiss, she writhed in humiliation. If she were completely honest with herself, her shame wasn't just because she'd inadvertently disturbed a pair of lovers. No, her shame was that she had believed Jack's declarations of interest in her. Had been flattered by his attentions. Had liked the message in his bold eyes. Had felt secretly smug at having captured the big man's notice.

And now she knew he'd been toying with her.

She'd heard there were men who needed to prove their masculinity and did so by collecting women—the way she'd heard Indians collected scalps.

She tried to stifle her groan, but Phillip stirred, mumbled, "You all right?"

Lillian froze. "Yes," she barely breathed the word. When she was sure he was asleep again she slowly scooted down past his feet and scooted out from under the wagon, this time onto the grass inside the corridor between the wagons. She sat up, tossed her long braid over her shoulder, and leaned back against the nearest metal-rimmed wooden wheel. Bending her nightgown-covered legs and folding her arms around them, she sighed and dropped her head to her knees, closing her eyes on a fresh wave of humiliation.

Something dropped to the ground beside her.

Like a bolt of lightning, panic streaked through her limbs. But her instinct to jump up and run was halted by a hand on her arm and an almost imperceptible soft drawl, "Don't go, Miss Lily Ann."

Her head came up. "Why—what . . ." she sputtered. Jack—again!

"I need to talk to you . . . to tell you that what you saw—"

"I don't have to listen to you," she hissed.

He interrupted her. "But I need to explain."

Lillian scrambled away from Jack and dived back under the sheet into the darkness beneath the wagon.

Jack stood at the spot where she'd disappeared. His low whisper was clear, "You misunderstood, Miss Lily Ann."

Lillian remained motionless until she heard his footsteps retreating. Then she rolled on her side, muttering to herself under her breath, "Of all the nerve. As if who Jack Montgomery kisses matters to me." She clutched the fingers of her left hand tightly in her right hand, her thumb and index finger settling on her wedding ring. "After all, I'm a married woman. And Jack is a heathen."

CHAPTER TWELVE

When the sentry's gun sounded the usual wake-up call two mornings later, Lillian opened her eyes and looked around under the wagon, squinting in the dim light. Phillip's blankets were folded back—just the way she'd left them for him the night before. She smiled; he'd never done that before.

"Phillip will make a wonderful father," she whispered happily to herself, running her hands over her rounded abdomen. She never failed to feel thrilled over the coming child.

Lillian donned her flowered dress, folded and stowed the bedding in the wagon, and set about preparing breakfast. Although Phillip hadn't yet made an appearance, she refused to be worried; he was no doubt seeing to their oxen or conferring with the men.

As daylight illuminated the campsite, Lillian looked around at her fellow travelers preparing for the day. She had to admit she was beginning to feel a bit anxious; she could see that every man was accounted for at his own wagon. So where was Phillip?

She looked up from the bowl of pancake batter to see Tomas running toward her, calling, "Buenos dias, Senora Denbeigh. Have you seen Senorita Desiree this morning?"

"Good morning, Sir. No, I haven't seen her," she called back as he darted past, headed toward Jack's wagons.

Lillian set Phillip's coffee cup and his plate piled with pancakes and crisp bacon on the spring seat. As she turned to take care of the fire, she noticed Jack and Tomas moving toward the Sanders's wagon. When she'd extinguished the flames, she looked up to see the two men striding toward her.

Glancing around her campsite, Jack said curtly, "Where's the Reverend?"

"I-I don't know." Lillian's voice quavered despite her determination not to sound worried.

"What do you mean, you don't know," he barked at her, his brown eyes boring into hers.

When tears threatened to betray her anxiety, Lillian stiffened her back and retorted sharply, "Just what I said—I don't know. I—he hasn't been—he was gone when I got up this morning—" her voice wobbled again. She cleared her throat, trying desperately to ignore the anxious thoughts attacking her mind.

"Were you awake when he came to bed last night?" Jack's voice had gentled.

"N-no." She shook her head. "He said he was going to visit with Mr. Sanders."

"Did you wake up in the night?"

Again she shook her head. "No. A-And he was gone when I woke this morning." She frowned, "Is—Is Miss Vargas missing—too?

At Jack's nod, she whispered, "You don't think . . ?"

"I don't think anything . . . yet." Jack touched her arm, suggested, "Why don't you go back and wait with Maria while we finish making the rounds of the wagons. She could use your company."

Lillian stared after the two men as they strode past Tomas's wagon and stopped to talk to Isaac Prewitt.

Lillian took several deep breaths in an effort to control the sick feeling swelling in the pit of her stomach—a nauseous "knowing" that something terrible had happened. The light wind blowing from the direction of the cattle brought with it a "farm" smell that compounded her indigestion.

She walked toward the Velasquez wagon—maybe visiting with Maria would be a good distraction—but she hadn't taken more than ten steps when Jack and Tomas came hurrying back.

Maria climbed down from the wagon to join Lillian and the two men; she stood beside Lillian, sniffing repeatedly as she prayed her rosary beads under her breath.

"You two stay here," Jack addressed Maria and Lillian. "Tomas and I will take a couple of my horses and ride back along the trail to see if there are any signs of them." Even though Jack didn't say the words out loud, they all knew he really meant "signs of an Indian attack."

Maria's face crumpled and she started to cry. Lillian felt like weeping too, but she bit her lips between her teeth and slipped her arm around Maria. When she could speak without giving way to her emotions, she said, "Come, Maria, let's go sit on the spring seat of your wagon."

An hour later Jack and Tomas returned to the campsite. Maria jumped down as they approached, but Lillian, feeling weak and shaken, remained on the bench. The men reported that they'd ridden more than a mile in each direction, examining the trail on both sides, searching for footprints, blood—anything that would indicate foul play. But they had found nothing.

Upon hearing the news, Maria burst out, "This is all my fault. Tomas didn't want to bring Desiree—he said she was trouble. But I insisted." She sniffed and squeezed her beads. "She's my own cousin. I'm her only family. I thought we should help her. You know—that maybe she would meet a nice man and get married." She sniffed again. "But no! She runs off with a married man . . ."

As Maria's words dissolved into a wail, her assumption that Phillip and Desiree had run off together startled Lillian, scraping raw her already taut nerves. She leaped up from the wagon bench, her blue eyes blazing hot sparks as she lashed out at Maria, "If you think my Phillip ran off with Miss Vargas, you're crazy!" She sputtered, "Phillip would never do such a thing! Why he-he—" Her voice rose until she was shouting. "How could you even think such a despicable thing?"

Sobbing wildly, Maria cowered in the face of Lillian's outrage. Tomas, however, wrapped his arm around his wife's trembling shoulders and turned on Lillian. His eyes flashed and his words were hard and cold. "They were last seen talking together last night, so Maria's not as crazy as you might think."

Jack glared at Tomas, as if to say, Don't make matters worse. Then he reached up to Lillian and helped her to the ground. "Come," he said, insistently propelling her toward her own wagon.

Too angry and frightened to think straight, she twisted away from him.

Jack tried to reason with her. "All this excitement can't be good for Junior, now can it?"

Lillian darted a last reproachful glance back at Tomas and Maria but they weren't paying any attention to her; Tomas was holding his wife, who was hysterically pounding his chest with her fists, her beads slapping him with each blow.

"Wha-what do you think happened?" Lillian asked when she'd finally recovered her composure. "Is-is what Tomas said—about last night—is it true?" She had herself enough in hand to realize she had to face the facts, whatever they might be.

"I don't know, Miss Lily Ann. I just don't know." Jack lifted his hat and ran his fingers through his mahogany curls. "I do know—" he sucked in a hollow breath and made a wry face as he smashed his hat back on his head, "I do know that Miss Vargas was . . . ah . . . too forward with nearly every man in the wagon train at one time or another."

Lillian threw him a skeptical sideways glance. Was he trying again to tell her that Desiree had come onto him the other night when she'd seen them kissing under the oak tree? She shook her head. No, she knew what she'd seen. Desiree may have been unpopular with the women, but that didn't excuse Jack.

Jack answered the disbelief in her eyes. "The other night—what you saw—that was one of her many attempts with me." His mouth was grim. "For your benefit, I might add."

Her sneering lips proclaimed her doubt before she mocked, "Oh, stop lying to me!"

He held up his hand. "It's the truth."

"And you think—you think Miss Vargas enticed my Phillip and—and just like that—" she snapped her fingers, "convinced him to run away with her?" She ground her teeth and growled, "I *know* Phillip. He would never do such a thing. It's just not in his nature. Why, he turned down a prestigious position with a big church in Boston to come west to minister to needy people." She shook her head. "No, I can't believe it; he's a man of unshakeable integrity. There has to be some other explanation."

Jack eyed her quizzically. "Miss Lily Ann," he said her name in a patient whisper, "there isn't any other explanation. There are no signs of foul play, no Indian tracks, no signs of a struggle, no bodies. The only explanation is that they ran off together. We are, after all, only three days' journey out of Fort Hall."

"Three days' journey is a long way on foot, Jack Montgomery!" she retorted sharply, her eyes burning with indignation.

Jack balled his fists and turned his back on her.

He was silent so long that Lillian demanded, "What?" She gave his arm a sharp tug. "What aren't you telling me?"

He swung around. "Two of my horses are missing, Miss Lily Ann." He shifted from one foot to the other. "Phillip and Desiree are no doubt half way back to Fort Hall even as we speak."

"Then I'm going after them," Lillian declared flatly. "I'll find them and—and Phillip will come to his senses and—and—"

"And what? Come back with you?" Jack shook his head. "No, Miss Lily Ann. Your faith in Phillip is most commendable—but you are certainly naive." He pressed his mouth into a grim line. "No man would welcome that kind of confrontation."

Lillian averted her face. She blinked and swallowed hard. Defeat was a foreign concept and disgrace was to be avoided at all costs. How could Phillip have done this to her? How could God have let it happen?

As another thought struck her, she gasped and stomped her foot. "I'm carrying Phillip's child. Do you know how much he wanted a son? I can't believe—no, it cannot be true—there has to be another explanation."

Jack just stood there. She read the pity in his eyes; he truly believed Phillip and Desiree had run off together. And he felt sorry for her.

Lillian's body grew rigid as the hardship and horror of the past five months rushed over her. The heat, the cold, the tasteless food, the burned fingers and raw knuckles, the pain, the insanity, the tragedy, the death—it had all been for nothing. The flickers of smoldering bitterness erupted into a conflagration that turned every trace of faith into ashes and left her soul a charred, desolate shell—just like the wildfire had scorched the land.

When she finally spoke, her voice held no emotion—it sounded dead, even to her own ears. "Well, then I shall have to go on without him. Make a new life for myself." The light died in her face, her eyes became empty black holes. "How soon do we leave, Mr. Montgomery?"

Jack flinched at the hardness in her tone. "You're not—you can't drive this wagon by yourself, Miss Lily Ann; not in your condition. Let me . . ."

The unfamiliar, dead voice interrupted harshly, "Oh, yes, I can. And I certainly will."

"I was going to offer to drive it for you at the front of the train."

"No need." Lillian's voice was as frigid as a mountain stream. "The worst is behind us. I'll do it myself." She glared at him.

"All right, all right!" Jack lifted his hands in a gesture of surrender, "Have it your way. We leave in fifteen minutes. Be ready." He turned on his heel and stalked off.

CHAPTER THIRTEEN

Dry cornbread for breakfast that tasted as old as buffalo chips, accompanied by the farm smell emanating from her oxen, made Lillian gag—but in spite of her aching weariness, Lillian refused to entertain Jack's offer to drive her wagon. She perched on her hope chest and stared out the front of the wagon until she saw the Sanford's wagon lurch forward. Then she scooted onto the spring seat and stood up. Grasping the whip by its handle, she swirled the lashes around and then imitated Phillip's snapping motion; she'd seen him do it at least twice a day since they'd set out from Independence—how hard could it be?

The long leather lashes sailed through the air and snapped back, striking her around the shoulders. Gutted of breath, her body slammed hard against the bench.

But in the next moment, she gritted her teeth and stood up again. She raised the whip in the air a second time. And this time she brought the lashes down hard on the oxen's backsides. They jerked, bellowing their protest, but Lillian steeled her heart against any feelings of mercy. When they started moving, she stiffened her jaw in stubborn satisfaction.

I am young. I am strong. I can make it on my own. Without Phillip. Without God.

Lillian's bitter thoughts became a litany that kept time with the oxen's rhythmic clomping.

When the train halted for the nooning, Lillian climbed to the ground and looked after her oxen. Bella Sanders called to her from her wagon, "Lillian, honey, won't you join us for a bite to eat? I've got fresh butter to put on our bread—it's been churning all morning on the side of the wagon." Concern laced the older woman's voice as she eyed Lillian's rounded figure. "A bit of rest will do you good."

Bella's kind words only made Lillian angry. She snapped ungraciously, "No. I'm just fine. And I don't need a rest." She stomped on the wagon tongue and heaved herself into her wagon. Dropping down on her hope chest, she reached for the breadbox; bread and cheese would make a simple lunch. She wasn't that hungry, anyway.

Lillian's hope that the worst of the trail lay behind them in the Rockies couldn't have been father from reality. As the afternoon progressed, the trail through the Wasatch Mountains became increasingly treacherous, and by dusk the wagons were merely inching along over the rugged terrain.

When they finally stopped for the night, Lillian quickly tended her oxen and then climbed inside her wagon—she didn't want anybody asking how she was doing. She managed to swallow a few mouthfuls of cold beans and some leftover cornbread. Weariness screamed in every muscle of her body; it had taken all her strength to maintain a tight hold on the reins as the oxen strained to haul their heavy load uphill.

Grabbing up her quilt, Lillian turned the words face down. So much for God. For prayers. For faith. It was up to her now.

She'd had little time to think while driving the wagon; the treacherous trail had required her full attention, but she was determined to think through her situation before she went to sleep. However, her weary body took over despite her intentions, and she was asleep before she had time to fight it.

When the gun blasted its early wake-up call, she sat up and looked around, momentarily disoriented. "Phillip?" Her voice sounded scratchy and hollow in her own ears.

Then awful reality hit her with a new dimension of cynicism: *Phillip ran off and left me pregnant and alone in the wilderness. So much for his grand talk about starting a church. Or ministering to the miners. He left me for another woman—after I rejected the suit of wealthy James Sinclair and broke my parents' hearts to follow him to the ends of the earth. He didn't even care enough to stay with me for the sake of his unborn child.*

Resentment ate at her soul.

I trusted Phillip. I trusted God. I even gave up my special quilt for a dead baby . . . and look where it got me. What a trusting fool I've been.

And while her mind rehearsed her caustic thoughts, Lillian relentlessly worked as hard as any man. She wedged rocks behind the wheels of her wagon to relieve the strain on her oxen as they pulled the wagon up the trail's sharp incline, and she managed the heavy rope and pulley to winch her wagon over the steepest spots. But in spite of her physical exertion, disillusionment soured her appetite.

* * *

By the evening of the third day after Phillip's and Desiree's disappearance, the wagons had inched their way safely down the other side of the pass. However, although the trail became less hazardous with every passing mile, the temperature grew increasingly hot and the air became desert dry.

Jack, keeping a close eye on Lillian from a distance, observed that her face looked drawn and she hadn't bothered to change her clothes or care for her hair since Phillip's disappearance.

Worried, not only for Lillian's sake but also for that of her unborn child, Jack deliberately slowed the pace of the wagons. It was a decision that involved great risk; delay could mean the difference between life and death for the children and adults depending on him.

After the wagons crossed the shallow, scummy remains of the Humbolt River in the late afternoon on the fourth day, a sharp, nasty wind came up. The wagon wheels threw up arid, gritty soil that blasted everything and everyone. Like a thick blanket, choking dust smothered the air. By the following morning some of the cattle were dead. Others showed signs of sickness.

Blood dripped from the nose of one of her oxen

when Lillian went to hitch up her teams. She hastily retrieved one of Phillip's shirts and tried unsuccessfully to staunch the blood. The ox sank to its knees, gave a low bellow, and then collapsed, dead. A few minutes later a second ox choked to death on its own blood.

Moving from wagon to wagon, Jack saw Lillian's first ox stumble and he heard its feeble bellow before it collapsed. As he dashed across the grass toward her, he heard the gurgling as the second ox choked and then plunged to the ground. He put one hand on Lillian's shoulder and reached with the other for the bloody shirt she was kneading between her tense fingers. A surge of hope flashed through him that this tragedy would shatter the harshness she'd adopted toward life; if only she'd yell at him—or cry—instead of denying her feelings.

His voice deliberately cool, he questioned matter-of-factly, "What do you plan to do, Miss Lily Ann?"

"Lighten my load," her scorn dashed his hope that her hard shell would crack, "and drive with one pair." If looks could fry, he would have sizzled like bacon.

Taking the wadded, bloody shirt with him, Jack turned on his heel and strode away. "I'll be back," he called to her over his shoulder as he headed toward the Sanders wagon to check on their livestock.

* * *

Lillian hoisted her pregnant body into her wagon. Wielding the crowbar Phillip had brought along, she pried up the lid on the crate of hymnals, grimaced at the once-loved smell of paper and ink, and began tossing the heavy, hard-cover books out the back of the wagon—as if to say she could certainly live without such reminders of her foolish faith.

With each toss she raged, "That's for you, Phillip! And that! And that!"

By the time Jack returned, she had finished with the hymnals, tossed out the lilac bush when the branches kept slapping her in the face, and progressed to the next crate. Shocked to see Bibles flying out the back end of Lillian's wagon, Jack approached from the side to avoid being hit. Pushing up an edge of the canvas bonnet, he demanded, "What on earth are you doing, Miss Lily Ann?"

"Lightening my load, of course," she snapped, obstinately refusing to look at him. She reached for another Bible. "With only one yoke of oxen, something has to go."

"Well, I was thinking you could use . . ." he began to offer one of his back-up yoke of oxen.

She reared back and glared at him. "I don't recall asking you what you think, Mr. Montgomery. Now kindly leave me alone." She shoved back the straggling hair falling in her face.

Jack didn't reply. He dropped the edge of the bonnet and set about harnessing her remaining yoke of oxen. When he finished, he turned to find her sitting ramrod-stiff on the spring seat.

Averting her gaze, she muttered an ungracious

"Thank you" and snatched the reins he handed up to her.

* * *

Jack took it slow that morning. He mentioned briefly to the men that Henry was doing repair on one of his wagons and would catch up by the time they stopped for the nooning. The party made good time that day and camped for the night at the Humbolt Sink, so named because at that point the increasingly narrow and muddy trickle of the Humbolt River ceased to exist, fading away into the parched earth.

With darkness came a welcome chill. But by early morning the heat was again rising off the desert in shimmering waves. Little did the weary travelers know that fifty miles of scorching sun and hot desert sand lay ahead of their beleaguered company.

At noon Jack watched Lillian stagger away from her wagon to take care of personal needs. Moving quickly, he deliberately struck up a conversation with George Sanders and stood where he could observe Lillian's return.

As she approached her wagon, she put her hand to her head and blinked rapidly as if trying to clear her vision. In the next moment she crumpled to the ground in a limp heap.

Jack was instantly beside her. He slid his arms under her thin frame and called out, "Sanders! Make a comfortable place for her inside her wagon."

George mounted the wagon tongue and leaned over the spring seat to peer inside. "A bed's already made up, Sir."

"Good. I'll move her wagon to the front of the train and hook up a second yoke of oxen; I'll drive it myself and get the youngest Prewitt boy to drive my second wagon."

"Quite right, Sir. Quite right."

"Run ahead to my wagons and let Henry know about the change in plans. And tell Barsina I need a jug of water. Bring it back with you— and be quick!"

Jack lifted Lillian into the wagon and knelt, placing her on her quilt. She lay so white and still that his heart felt caught in a vice. He folded one corner of the blanket over her legs, startled to read **PATIENCE** embroidered in pink.

At that moment the babe in her womb gave a hearty kick—and then a second one.

Moved in the deepest core of his being, Jack impulsively reached out his hand and placed it lightly on Lillian's abdomen. As if the child felt his hand, it gave another kick.

Lillian opened her eyes, surprising a look of wonder on Jack's face. Instantly, he snatched his hand back, his countenance resuming its stern demeanor. He forestalled any comment by speaking first, "So—you've decided to stay in the land of the living?"

"What am I doing here?" Lillian demanded, obviously displeased.

"You fainted," he said tersely.

"Yes, well, I'm fine now." Lillian tried to sit up but she was so weak she could only groan. She dropped back against the bedding.

"Fine, are you? I think not," Jack growled. "I'll be driving your wagon at the head of the train from now on, Miss Lily Ann. And I won't be tolerating any nonsense."

"Why, you—you . . !" Faint color surged in her cheeks but she lacked the strength to challenge him.

"Lie still and be quiet," he ordered as he disappeared out the front.

* * *

The Nevada desert seemed to stretch interminably. As water became an increasingly scarce commodity, each family carefully rationed drinking water. In spite of the physical grime caused by the heat and dust, no one wasted a single drop on hygiene. And the cattle went without food or drink for two days. Rattlesnakes infested the sagebrush, rearing and rattling as the wagons passed. Hungry coyotes trailed behind the wagons, ready to snatch up any abandoned morsel or unattended animal, and at night their eerie howling scraped on everyone's already frayed nerves.

As the demoralized party began the climb up the eastern slopes of the Sierra Nevada Mountains, the joy of discovering an occasional trickling mountain stream and the gradual relief from the heat were soon lost in the greatest challenge yet. For seventy miles the wagons had to be hoisted up with ropes, chains, winches, and pulleys—and then blocked, one wagon at a time, every few feet as they inched their way down. They did not dare stop; each day was a race against the winter snow that would soon descend on the rugged mountains and make them impassable.

The only major mishap through this death trap was the loss of one of Mr. Prewitt's wagons that careened over a cliff when the holding chain towing it behind his lead wagon snapped. Although the loss of the wagon and the supplies it carried was disheartening, for once, illness proved a blessing; the Prewitt boy who'd been driving the wagon was sick and riding in their front wagon at the time. The train rolled on as if nothing had happened.

Although Lillian recovered from her exhaustion, Jack now had the upper hand, and he adamantly refused to allow her to drive her own wagon. But that proved a blessing; as her abdomen continued to expand with her progressing pregnancy, her clothing no longer fit and she didn't want to be seen. She finally resorted to cutting up one of her flowered sheets and fashioning a larger dress for herself.

The last one hundred miles wound steadily down the Sierra Nevada's twisting western slopes. Mountain streams again provided welcome refreshment for the bone-weary travelers and their few scrawny surviving animals.

One evening, while the party camped on a grassy slope near a stream that rippled through a narrow meadow surrounded by birch, oak, and pine trees, Jack took it upon himself to provide maintenance for Lillian's wagon.

"What exactly are you doing?" she challenged Jack, returning to her wagon after seeing to her personal needs. While she'd been away, he had propped the wagon on his own jack and was busy removing a wheel.

"I noticed this morning that a couple of your wheels are as flaky and dry as old parchment. They need a good soaking," he answered pleasantly.

At the disbelief in her eyes, he explained, "The desert heat has made the wood so brittle it's only a matter of time before one of them breaks. I'm going to take them off and soak them in the stream."

He removed the metal band from the first wheel and laid it to one side. While he rolled the wheel to a nearby birch tree and leaned it against the trunk, Lillian moved to the front of the wagon and climbed down. She stood off to the side, safely out of the way, watching in silence.

But when Jack dropped to his knees beside the second wheel, she moved to the tree, grasped the wooden wheel, pulled it upright, and began rolling it toward the stream. It was large and very heavy, and it wobbled, threatening to veer in the wrong direction at every rock and hole.

"What the—!" Jack roared when he looked up and saw Lillian struggling to guide the awkward wheel.

Startled by his shout, Lillian lost control. The wheel fell on her, knocking her down and thumping her on the head when it pinned her to the ground.

Jack swore fiercely and rushed to Lillian's aid. He grabbed the heavy wheel by the spokes and tossed it aside like a child's toy. In the next moment, he was on his knees beside Lillian, smoothing her hair back from her face, feeling for the lump on her head with gentle fingers.

"For goodness sake, I'm just fine," Lillian protested, shoving him away. "If you hadn't yelled at me, I'd be to the river by now."

Jack's mouth hardened into a harsh line. "Even if you don't care about yourself, think about Junior."

Lillian got to her feet, straightened her back and shoulders, and sniped at him. "I'll thank you to mind your own business, Jack Montgomery."

Obviously she was in no mood to be appealed to for the sake of herself or her unborn child. He tried a different approach. "Look, how you treat yourself or your—your child," he gestured toward her rounded figure, "really isn't my concern. But if you have that baby too soon, I'll have to stop the wagons for digging a grave—or maybe two." He saw her flinch but he didn't allow it to deter him. "And we really can't spare the time. Now, go back to your wagon and sit under those trees," he stabbed a forefinger toward the cluster of tall birches near her wagon, "and stay there!" His set jaw left no room for argument.

Lillian rolled her eyes at him but she headed back toward the shading tree without further dispute.

Heaving an exasperated groan, Jack rolled the

wheel down to the water's edge. He cast quick, frequent glances back up toward Lillian to confirm that she was indeed following his orders, and he almost turned back when she put her hand to her head and gingerly explored it with her fingers.

When she finally sat down, closed her eyes, and leaned her head back against the tree trunk, Jack exhaled a longsuffering sigh of relief.

CHAPTER FOURTEEN

Seven months and eighteen days . . . so much for the promise that the journey west would take five months at the outside. Lillian stood on an embankment and looked down on the verdant Sacramento valley that was to be her new home. Today would be the last day of the journey. While everyone else in their little camp was rejoicing because they had made it safely to the "Promised Land," Lillian's heart sat in her chest like a cold chunk of marble. Sacramento had been Phillip's choice, not hers.

A rescue team with pack mules hauling food and supplies had come up from Sacramento three days ago. As she'd listened to the rescuers relate the horrific tales of other parties, Lillian had disdainfully curled her lip. One party had lost half of its eighty-two members; well, so had she—half of two is one!

The awe-inspiring view did nothing for Lillian's pessimistic thoughts. *Never again will I allow myself to get attached to anything or anyone. People can't be trusted. Even God failed me. It's up to me to take care of myself. Oh, if only I weren't pregnant. What an inconvenient time to be stuck with a baby.*

As the wagons followed the dirt trail into Sacramento and headed toward a vacant field where they would set up a temporary camp, Lillian looked around with intent interest. Tents and hovels dotted the landscape along either side of the road that led to a six-block stretch of wood houses and fanned out away from the river with new construction.

And then it came to her: she would establish a boarding house with the money her parents had sent with her to help her and Phillip get settled in Oregon. She could do most of the work herself . . .

The baby kicked her ribs, sending her grand plans crashing into harsh reality. *How can I do anything with a squalling infant?*

* * *

Jack stopped by Lillian's wagon the next day to check on her, but she was nowhere to be found. He had deliberately waited until nearly noon to come by, thinking—hoping—she would take advantage of the opportunity to get some much-needed rest. Well, so much for his attempt to be thoughtful. He sat down in the shade of her wagon, determined to wait.

Two hours later, she came walking along the dirt street toward the camp, her bonnet swinging from her fingers by its ribbons. Watching her approach, Jack's heart gave a leap—maybe here she would forget her past troubles and return to the buoyant-spirited young woman she'd been when he'd first met her.

"I came by to say good-morning," Jack said, jumping up to meet her when she reached her wagon, "but it looks like you got an early start to your day."

"I did," she replied shortly, offering no further explanation and avoiding his eyes.

Jack raised one eyebrow. "All right. You obviously don't want to talk about it."

"That's right. I don't." She stepped up on the wagon tongue.

Stung by her heartless attitude, he took a step closer, "You can shut everybody else out, Miss Lily Ann, but you can't shut me out. Wherever you turn, I'm going to be there."

"Men," she scoffed. "You're all alike. You think women can't get along without you."

* * *

Two days later, Lillian discovered that the building she'd set her heart on purchasing belonged to a leather-faced miner, Bert Jenks, who flatly refused to negotiate with a woman. She'd coaxed, fluttering her bonnet in her hands as coquettishly as if it were a fine ladies' fan—even pausing to peep at him around the edge with one eye covered as if she were winking at him. But to no avail. The harder she tried to charm him, the more obnoxious and belligerent he became.

Finally, Mr. Jenks informed her that he didn't need her money. He outlined further, in graphic, vulgar terms, what he thought the only use for women happened to be. He struck his final blow by letting his eyes slowly appraise her swollen figure. When he finished his bold assessment, he shook his shaggy head and rolled his eyes in disgust.

Lillian flushed at his crudeness but she willed herself to be tough. Lifting her chin, she stared at him through narrowed eyes. An idea had been born. *Money is not the only currency with which I can buy comfort and independence. Why toil away my youth in some miserable boarding house? There are other houses, or so I've heard, where luxury surrounds a woman and gives her control over the men who slavishly come seeking favors.*

She shrugged off her twinge of conscience and allowed her thoughts to follow their course.

Oh, if only I weren't pregnant!

In the next moment, pragmatic determination came to her rescue.

Pregnancy won't be a problem for long. I'll just find a couple, bereaved of their child or children, who will be overjoyed to take care of mine. Even some do-gooders who'll take this baby out of a sense of Christian duty will suit me just fine.

In response to the nagging guilt for her heartless attitude, she chewed on her lower lip and finally conceded that she would even consider paying them for their services.

Lillian's eyes burned with the intensity of her planning, and she gloated under her breath all the way back to her wagon. *There is more than one way to get what I want.*

Recognizing that she needed help to put her plan

into effect, she decided the best strategy was to enlist Jack's help. Immediately upon arriving back at her wagon, Lillian combed her hair and rubbed her cheeks and hands with a bit of the bag balm Jack had given her to use on her parched lips when she was sick.

True to his word that he would not leave her to herself, Jack showed up at noon, carrying a bowl containing enough stew for both of them.

Lillian looked up from the tray she had prepared and grinned to herself. She'd expected him to come by—and she was ready for him. She'd baked fresh biscuits, added a bit of water to the last of her jerky and simmered it until the appetizing aroma of spicy meat in its own gravy filled the air, and she'd rummaged through her supplies, procuring her last jar of currant jelly. She'd even spread out her quilt—face up, no less—on the grass near her wagon.

At her smile of welcome, she caught a speculative gleam in Jack's brown eyes. "What?" she exclaimed, quite as if she hadn't been abominably rude to him every time he'd tried to befriend her.

He cocked his head and shot her a shrewd look. "What do you want, Miss Lily Ann?"

"What do I want?" She had no trouble sounding shocked; she hadn't expected him to be so perceptive. She could see she'd have to feed his curiosity enough to obscure her real reason for abandoning her antagonism.

"Well, I've been thinking about the baby coming. ." Her pensive expression accomplished exactly what she intended; the accusatory light went out of his eyes. But when it was replaced with something warmer, something that made her flush, she dropped her eyes to the dirt she'd been pushing around with the toe of her shoe—she'd worn her best ones today, deciding she not only needed to play a part to get her way, she needed to look it—and swallowed quickly before continuing.

"I—" she put the right amount of hesitation into her words, "I'm going to need help." She furrowed her brow, raised her blue eyes to his, and did her best to infuse them with apology. "I've been pretty difficult to be around, I know," she confessed, then lowered her voice in appeal, "but I've decided to mend my ways."

Triumph shot through her veins; he was swallowing her line—she could see it in his face. His hands shook and he almost dropped the bowl of stew. He plopped it on the wagon bench and touched her shoulder gently. "You've had a rough time, little girl, but things are bound to get better. I'll do what I can to help out on a daily basis, and I'm sure Bella Sanders will be more than glad to assist you when your time comes."

Lillian's confidence multiplied as Jack served up the stew, topped it with the jerky sauce, and helped himself to two of her muffins generously spread with currant jelly. Completely dropping his guard, he filled her in on details about Sacramento, which she mentally filed away for her less-than-righteous endeavor. Meantime, she smiled and laughed, gratified by the progress of her scheme.

Later that afternoon Bella Sanders came over and presented her with a tin cup mounded with fresh blackberries that she'd picked off bushes near the edge of town. It was an obvious attempt to befriend Lillian, and she knew instantly that Jack had spoken to the older woman about their earlier conversation. It galled her to have to conform to social niceties to get the help she needed, but her pleasure over the berries was decidedly genuine.

"Thank you, Mrs. Sanders." She popped a plump blue-black berry in her mouth. "Mmm, I don't think I can eat just one!"

"Good girl," Bella approved. "It sure is nice to see you feeling more like your normal self. You had us pretty worried, my dear!"

"Yes, well, I'm doing my best to put the past behind me and look to the future." Lillian felt certain Bella Sanders had no idea what she meant, but she curved her mouth into a passable smile.

"Speaking of the future," Bella lowered her voice, "when your time comes, you can count on me; I've been the midwife for thirteen babies and helped with a dozen more." She reached out and patted Lillian's shoulder. "There's nothing quite as exciting as helping a new little one into the world."

Lillian couldn't help her cynical chuckle as she prepared for bed that night. *I have two people totally committed to helping me. Now if I can just find a family to take this baby, I can get on with my plans.*

* * *

The merciless sun beat down on her, and each day felt hotter than the day before. More than once Lillian almost despaired; the child now filled her body until she could hardly breathe, and she continually found herself gritting her teeth to silence the frequent sharp retorts that flooded her mind as Jack and Bella hovered over her. Oh, she would be glad when the problem of this baby was resolved. Not only had she not found a dutiful Christian family to take her child, she'd learned of at least a dozen other children who'd arrived in Sacramento as orphans.

Finally, in desperation, she broached the subject with Jack—and was astonished to learn he had a solution.

"Barsina has offered to watch Junior for you, Miss Lily Ann." He eyed her carefully before adding, "I've hesitated to tell you because she says God spoke to her and told her to help you out. Seems she's got religion— she and Henry have been going to the revival meetings in the mercantile with that preacher, Sam Winston."

Lillian nearly laughed out loud. Having Jack attribute Barsina's helpfulness to God—Jack, of all people!—was almost more than she could bear. She turned away to hide the scorn she couldn't mask.

So now it's God who is helping me! Of all the bizarre ideas . . . that God will tell someone to take care of my child so I can open a brothel.

"So what do you think about that, Miss Lily Ann?" Jack's voice interrupted her contemptuous thoughts.

She twisted her lips into a smile and forced herself

to say sweetly, "I think Barsina will do just fine, Jack. That's very generous of her, especially now that she has her freedom."

"Well, as a matter of fact, she and Henry are going to open a home for orphaned children. I put up the money to have supplies shipped from the East to build a house for them on a piece of property I purchased at the north end of town—right where the river comes around the bend."

Lillian's mouth sagged but she quickly caught herself. Jack was speaking about purchasing property—and he still thought she wanted to open a boarding house. Why not let him do the negotiating with Bert Jenks?

"Mr. Mont—Jack . . . ?" She quickly changed her salutation at the look on his face.

He raised his brows, "Hmm?"

"Would—do you think . . ?" She hesitated, dropping her lashes just the teensiest bit coquettishly.

"Go ahead; just say it." His soft, amused drawl eased her nerves and bolstered her courage.

"I want to buy the house that's for sale—the one that belongs to Bert Jenks. You know, the big three-story house at the south end of town." She held her breath.

"The one next to the saloon?" His eyes pierced to her soul like silver bullets but she steeled herself to meet them without flinching.

"I—yes, I guess it is next to the saloon." She rushed to add, "It's the only large house available, and being close to the saloon should be good for business . . . what I mean is, it won't be hard for people to find." Her muscles tensed until the baby kicked, giving her an excuse to look down. She had inadvertently almost given away her intentions. And even a man as heathen as Jack would object to her plans, of that she was certain.

"How do you propose to make such a purchase?"

"I—I have some money. My parents sent it with me. Of course I can't spend it all to purchase the house; I'll need some to get set up."

"I'll see what I can do," Jack promised.

Glad for the breeze that cooled her face, Lillian repressed her smirk. *Who needs God? I'm quite capable of managing my own affairs.*

CHAPTER FIFTEEN

Five and a half years later.

"It's Mr. Montgomery to see you, Madame Lily," announced Angelique, the stylish "lady" who also served as Lillian's assistant.

Seated on a curved-back chair upholstered in a delicate needlepoint tapestry and leaning her slender wrists on the kidney-shaped mahogany desk in her office in The Red Door, Lillian glanced up from the letter she'd been reading. The years had been kind; Lillian was far more beautiful in a polished sort of way than she had been as a girl-bride.

"Show him up," she instructed.

The Red Door had been successful—beyond Lillian's wildest dreams. The third floor housed her personal quarters, and she had gradually filled the bedroom, dressing room, and sitting room with lovely furnishings and accessories. The four "ladies" who worked for Madame Lily, as she called her aloof, reinvented self, lived very comfortably in two large rooms on the second floor, while a third room served as the kitchen. The ground floor had been remodeled into four small but lavishly decorated intimate bedrooms opening off a large parlor furnished with a pianoforte, two gold brocade-covered sofas, several side tables holding elegant gas lamps, and four wing backed chairs. Sumptuous rugs covered the hardwood floors, and striped wallpaper in two shades of pale green covered the parlor walls. Dark green moiré silk draperies framed the tall windows.

The Red Door was open for business four afternoons and six evenings each week, and although Lillian hosted a lavish party each Sunday evening, providing free food and drinks to all regular clients, that was the extent of her personal involvement with the patrons outside of keeping peace and calmly evicting unruly customers.

Every six months for the past five years, Jack Montgomery had paid a visit to Lillian with an offer to buy her out. She'd refused each time, always informing him in no uncertain terms that she enjoyed being the richest lady in town. Truth be told, she'd been surprised that Jack never gave up.

What Jack didn't know, however, was that today Lillian planned to take him up on his offer. Feeling almost giddy, she rose to her feet and rushed to her bedroom. She checked her appearance in the opulent gilt-framed mirror filling the wall behind her dressing table then squeezed the spritzing bulb on a pale blue lead crystal perfume bottle, enveloping her figure in imported scent.

* * *

All it took to distract Jack from the centuries-old Chinese vase displayed on Lillian's sideboard was the whisper of silk. He turned as she entered the room, and for a moment he stood transfixed.

With her rich chestnut hair twisted up and held in place with an elaborate pearl-encrusted clip and her slender body draped in a yellow silk gown whose soft folds clung to her every curve, she smiled warmly and swept up to him in a wave of sophisticated scent even as she graciously offered her hands. "Dear Jack. How nice to see you again."

Jack's eyes narrowed slightly—he knew her well, and she was up to something—she'd never before expressed pleasure over his visits. But he returned her smile, took her hands, and said what he always said, "Are you ready to become a respectable woman, Miss Lily Ann?"

"And how much are you willing to offer me today, Jack Montgomery?" She said it in the same laughing way she always said it.

But instead of playing the usual game of offer and counter offer, counter again, and a refusal thrown in his face, Jack, on a hunch, changed his tactics. "No offer today; I've offered for the last time." He shook his head, his voice cool. "It's time you decide to do what's right because it's right instead of because somebody offered to pay you to do it."

"Why . . . what's gotten into you, Jack Montgomery?" He saw that she almost lost her composure, but she made a quick comeback. "I thought you'd be asking me to sell out 'til my dying day," she teased, fluttering her lashes slightly.

"Well, you thought wrong, didn't you?" His amiable tone held a thread of steel.

She blinked at his challenge and then deliberately burned her bridges, "If you don't want to buy it, then I shall just have to find somebody else to take it off my hands. I had decided to take you up on your offer this time." She raised her long lashes and met his intent gaze. "I want to go back East. I've just received a letter from my mother, and even though she won't say it, her handwriting tells me she's not well."

He was silent for a long moment before he said, "Are you taking Grace with you?"

Lillian sucked in a sharp breath; they had never talked about her daughter. Henry and Barsina were raising Grace, along with nearly two dozen other orphans, and Lillian compensated her generously—but she never went to visit the child or in any way acknowledged her existence. She hadn't even bothered to name her—Barsina had done the honors.

"No, I'm not," she replied in a tight voice. "I've never told my parents about her, and besides, I can't imagine traveling with a child, much less one who doesn't even know me."

Emboldened by Lillian's candor, Jack pressed, "Oh, she knows you, Miss Lily Ann. Barsina has pointed you out to Grace on many occasions when you've passed the mercantile while they were shopping. She prays for you every night and she sleeps under your old quilt with the tattered corner that says LOVE tucked under her chin." He made a final, brutal thrust, "But then, I'm sure you wouldn't care about that either, would you?"

Lillian stared at him, her mouth opening and closing. Jack—heathen Jack—had just badgered her with her long-lost faith! She stalked to the door, flung it open, and called her assistant, "Angelique!"

When the young woman appeared in the hallway, Lillian gestured toward Jack. "Mr. Montgomery is leaving," she said coldly. "Please show him out."

CHAPTER SIXTEEN

Six months later.

From her seat in the stage coach, Lillian watched the driver, Mr. Horton, and his assistant, Toby, efficiently set up the two tents—just as they had each evening for the past three weeks. But today is different, she reminded herself.

"Tent's ready, Madam." Mr. Horton called to her, interrupting her thoughts.

Lillian leaned forward. "Thank you, Mr. Horton." Ignoring Toby's struggle to drag her heavy trunk across the dry grass, she took Mr. Horton's proffered hand and allowed him to assist her to the ground.

She smoothed her palms lightly over her pencil slim skirt, thinking as she did so that styles had certainly changed from the day she'd been so proud of that awful, homemade, deeply-flounced flowered dress with the refurbished bonnet she'd worn the last time she stood in this place—the one she'd personally and purposefully torched in her burn barrel!

An hour later, following a simple meal, the three travelers gathered around the campfire. Toby fished a tin of chewing tobacco from his coat's inner pocket. He opened the shiny container, took a pinch between his stained thumb and forefinger, and stuffed it in his cheek. Mr. Horton selected a cigar from a small wooden box he carried in his shabby waistcoat pocket and settled down for a smoke.

Lillian, who'd changed into a loose-fitting cotton dress, sat on an upended stump near the fire and stared morosely into the flames. Yes, today was different; today marked the sixth anniversary of Phillip's betrayal and disappearance. With the sale of The Red Door to a businessman new to Sacramento, she'd achieved financial security beyond her wildest imaginings.

Without Phillip.

Without God.

And she'd felt driven by a strong inclination to go back to the place where it all began . . . as if to say, See! I succeeded without either of you.

She frowned and sighed.

Both men eyed Lillian with idle curiosity—and not for the first time on this journey. But tonight, their curiosity reached a new height.

Mr. Horton cleared his throat noisily. "Ahem."

Lillian shifted her gaze to the stagecoach driver and raised her finely shaped eyebrows. "Did you wish to speak to me?" She lifted her chin slightly and looked down her nose; years of shrewd dealing with the underside of society had honed "the look" to an art.

Undeterred, Mr. Horton began, "Yes, Madam, I'm a wonderin'—" He tossed his cigar stub into the fire and cleared his throat again. "It's like this, Madam. No one in the three years I've been driving this trail has ever been so smartly particular as you." He tipped his grizzled, balding head. "So would you mind telling me why you wanted to stop here . . . precisely?"

Any attempt on Lillian's part to answer Mr. Horton's question was drowned out by a sing-song, thick-brogue voice accompanied by a rattling that sounded like tin pans banging against each other as the person owning the voice approached the campfire through the darkness.

"Come and tell me, Sean O'Farrell,
Tell me why you hurry so.
Hush, me boy, now hush and listen;
And his eyes were all aglow.
I bear orders from the captain,
Get you ready quick and soon,
For the pikes must be t'gether
By the risin' o' the moon.

By the risin' o' the moon,
By the risin' o' the moon,
For the pikes must be t'gether
By the risin' o' the moon . . ."

Mr. Horton's hand moved to rest on his pistol as he called out, "Who goes there?"

The slightly off-key rendition of the Irish rebel's ballad turned into a chuckle as a spindly-legged, bony creature with long, matted hair, a bushy beard, and beady eyes emerged from the shadows. The wiry, rag-clad figure dropped his lumpy satchel on the ground in a final discordant clanging. He unceremoniously followed it down to sit cross-legged on the ground by their fire.

"Ev'nin', ev'nin'," the stranger greeted with another chuckle. "Darby Carter's the name. Miner's the trade." He flashed an almost toothless grin. "Mind ye if I sit—an' warm me'self by yer spit?"

Lillian's lips twitched with disgust and she quickly covered her nose with her lavender scented linen handkerchief.

Mr. Horton's booming voice welcomed the man. "What's the news, Mr. Carter?" He raised his brows, "Not much mining around here these days, is there?"

When Darby chuckled again, Lillian decided that between his chuckling and his rhyming he at least provided an interesting diversion from her dark thoughts. The triumph she had expected to feel in returning to this place a supremely successful woman had somehow escaped her, so this odd little man offered a welcome distraction to the haunting ache squeezing her heart in its merciless grip.

Darby's gnarled, dirty fingers with their broken nails reached out and retrieved his satchel. Fumbling with the drawstrings, he replied, "Oh, I make it up to these 'ere parts every so often. I 'spect I'll keep on comin' 'til they put me in a coffin."

His head bobbed and his untidy hair formed a grimy curtain around his face. He chuckled and stretched open the mouth of his satchel. Thrusting his hand inside, he shuffled the contents with much rattling. A charger used for panning gold was the first item to emerge in Darby's fist, and he plunked it on the ground beside his bony frame.

"Found things in me wandrin', show ya sunthin' interestin'?" He didn't wait for a response, just reached again into his satchel and shifted the contents noisily. "Want to 'ear a Bible storee, better'n the one 'bout Noahee?" With a cackle, he extracted a rectangular object wrapped in a piece of stained, faded calico.

Put off by Darby's reference to the Bible, Lillian started to rise, intending to retreat to her tent, but when the cloth slid down Darby's arm and exposed a leather-bound Bible with gilt edged pages that, although water-streaked and faded, still glinted in the firelight, she sank back down on the log with a thump.

Toby spoke up, "Sure, Darby. Spin us a yarn 'bout how you got converted." He guffawed at his own joke.

"Sing a song, ya got it wrong," Darby taunted with his missing-teeth grin. "I found this here holy tome, a-lyin' on a dead man's bones."

Lillian felt her body go cold.

Darby continued his rhyming as he handed the Bible to Mr. Horton. "Readin's not for me, but ye can see what ye can see."

Mr. Horton grasped the sacred book and squatted by the fire. Taking care not to break the binding, he raised the stiff leather cover and then peeled back the pages until he reached the presentation page. With the book held out at arm's length, he squinted to read the inscription. "Presented to Phillip Arthur Denbeigh—"

Lillian shrieked and toppled off the stump into the dirt in a dead faint.

Her three companions exhibited various manifestations of shock. Mr. Horton dropped the Bible in the dirt and was on his knees beside her in an instant, frantically patting her white face. Darby Carter leaped in the air, slapping his thighs and exclaiming, "By all that's Irish!" And Toby jumped up, accidentally kicking the gold-mining charger, which banged and echoed in several mighty gongs when it slammed against the closest log and then gyrated in the dirt.

Lillian regained consciousness to find the peering eyes in three worried, wizened faces hovering above her. Mr. Horton was furiously fanning her with the charger while Toby spasmodically pumped her right hand—as if he expected that would somehow promote her circulation and revive her. Behind them, Darby Carter's head bobbed as he exclaimed, "Well, gory be! What's wi' ye?"

Lillian struggled to sit up, reaching her right hand to rub the back of her head where it had struck a fallen tree limb when she fainted.

As the three men backed away, Mr. Horton quickly inquired, "Are you quite all right, Madam?"

Ignoring the solicitous question, Lillian demanded, "Let me see that book." She pointed at the Bible Mr. Horton had dropped in the drama of the moment and which now lay face down, its pages crumpled in the dirt.

Darby bent his spindly legs to retrieve the Bible. He smoothed the pages with his dirty fingers, and when he seemed satisfied that none were torn he closed the cover and scraped the book, front first and then the back, across his shirt to dust off the grit. "Here ye be, Miss-ee."

Lillian lifted the cover, turned to the presentation page, and read the faded words for herself. "Where did you find this?" she demanded in a thin voice, her eyes narrowed and steaming with accusation.

"Up the trail—to the west," Darby gestured with his thin arm, "a'lyin' on a dead man's chest." He reached down and began poking around in his satchel again. "Also foun' this gent'man's ring. Ain't it a rightly pretty thing?" Darby extended his hand and opened it to display a man's gold wedding band resting on his grimy palm.

Before he could say another word, Lillian's hand struck out and she snatched up the ring.

"Gory be, be nice to me!" he screeched at her, recoiling as if she'd struck him.

"Be quiet," Lillian snapped. She clutched the Bible close to her chest with one hand and squeezed the ring between the thumb and forefinger on her other. Jumping to her feet, she darted close to the flames and crouched so the firelight illuminated the inner band of the circlet.

Her body started to shake—it was indeed Phillip's wedding ring; the initials LC.PD were clearly engraved inside. She sank to a stump and demanded through white lips and chattering teeth, "Tell me all you know about this book and this ring."

Darby gulped, sending his Adam's apple bobbing up and down in his scrawny, chicken-neck throat. His eyes bulged as he stammered, "What I know, I already tol'. On the gent'man's bony finguh, the golden ring did linguh. The book was on them bones; there was no heap 'o stones. The skull was wearin' a gash, where a tomeehawk smashed."

Upon hearing the last piece of information, Lillian sprang up so quickly she swayed and nearly fell. Flinging out one arm, she found her balance. With the Bible crushed to her chest and the ring clutched in her white-knuckled fist, she demanded ruthlessly, "You're telling me the whole truth?"

"Gory be, M'am, a' course I am. I got no why to be tellin' a lie."

"No, I suppose you don't." Lillian's voice lost its intensity. She sank to the ground in a limp heap, quite as if the life had gone out of her. Wrapping her arms around the Bible and clasping it tightly to her heart, she began to wail. Her low groans took on a momentum that escalated until her cries echoed off the surrounding hills.

"Oh, God, oh, God, oh, God!"

As her cries grew into hysterical shrieks, the three men stared at her in open-mouthed panic.

Finally, Mr. Horton approached her cautiously and knelt in the dirt next to her. In a deliberately gentle voice, he soothed, "There, there, Madam. Calm yourself, calm yourself."

Although Lillian continued to stare at him through

swollen, stricken eyes, her shrill wailing gradually subsided to low cries. With trembling fingers she retrieved her handkerchief from her sleeve and wiped her face. Her cries eventually faded into sniffling and moans punctuated by hiccups.

When she finally had her emotions back under control, she looked around. Seeing the three men's frightened faces, she scraped out a terse explanation. "My husband and I were on our way to Sacramento with a train of wagons. Six years ago tonight, in this very place, Phillip and a woman from the train disappeared, along with two horses. Everyone believed they ran off together because no evidence could be found indicating Indian activity. I desperately didn't want to believe Phillip had betrayed me, but it seemed the only possible explanation. I've been angry at God ever since." She made a wry face, "No, worse than that, I've been bitter and wicked. I opened a brothel—and even gave away our baby," she hiccupped loudly and swiped again at her eyes.

"But Phillip was not unfaithful," a tremor shook her whole body, "he was murdered." She hung her head, sending fresh tears of remorse, regret, and repentance dripping onto Phillip's leather-bound Bible that now rested on her knees.

CHAPTER SEVENTEEN

Four months later.

Eyeing the closed gate in the white picket fence, Lillian felt the lump in her throat swell like a wad of wet cotton wool. She tried to swallow but it wouldn't go down. She'd written to tell her parents she was coming for a visit, but of course she couldn't give them an exact arrival date; transportation from the west was still unpredictable.

"Please, God, help me," she begged through stiff lips as she reached over the gate and lifted the latch.

Stepping onto the flagstones that led to the wide Victorian porch of her childhood home, Lillian had a flashback of her wedding day—coming down those steps on her father's arm and circling around to the lawn in back, where Phillip waited impatiently for his first glimpse of her, his innocent, trusting bride in her pristine white gown.

The memory faded as she pressed her gloved hand to her lips. She blinked hard and straightened her shoulders. There was no going back; she was no longer that naïve, spoiled, eager girl.

Childhood memories buzzed through her head as she stopped at the front door. Always, she had walked right in. Never a need to knock; this was her home. But now. She felt like the prodigal—she *was* the prodigal! Heartache and hope danced in her fingers as she raised her hand and grasped the *fleur de lys* knocker.

Her fingers slipped off the ornate bronze lily as the door flew open. She had no time to wipe her eyes or make an explanation—loving arms wrapped her in a near-death grip. Her mother's heaving sobs resonated through Lillian's whole being, and the primal scent of familiar lemon bathing soap transported Lillian back to childhood, to a time when mother-love could make every wrong come right. Lillian rested her head against her mother's breast and her weeping harmonized with her mother's cries.

When their emotional storm subsided at last, Eleanor Cartwright relaxed her hold on her daughter and Lillian raised her head. But even while Lillian mopped her face with her ever-present handkerchief, her mother kept one hand on her daughter's shoulder, as if to reassure herself that her dear girl was indeed present in the flesh.

With Lillian's last sniff, Eleanor nodded at Nora, discreetly waiting with a tea tray. The servant bobbed her head and swiftly crossed the foyer.

"Come," her mother urged Lillian. "Your father is in the parlor. He's insisted on dressing and sitting in his chair each day since we received your letter—to wait for you."

Her mother led the way down the hallway without giving Lillian a chance to ask about her father's health, but as she followed, she observed her mother's slowed steps and dragging left foot. Why had her mother never mentioned their health struggles in her newsy, cheerful letters?

"Dadda," Lillian used her affectionate childhood name for her father as she darted across the parlor. Dropping to her knees beside his chair, she reached out her arms and pulled him into a tight hug. When he lifted a shaking hand and patted her head, the same indulgent caress she remembered so well, she buried her nose in his waistcoat, relishing the smell of the horehound lozenges he always sucked to refresh his breath. She felt as if the "balm of Gilead" had indeed been applied to her soul.

When Lillian was at last settled next to her mother on the sofa, she twisted her damp handkerchief between her fingers and started at the beginning, recounting the triumphs and hardships of life on the trail. She got a chuckle when she confessed her first crooked bread slices and a groan when she told about collecting and cooking over the infamous "meadow muffins." When she mentioned baby Elizabeth's death and told how her quilt had been accidentally used as a shroud in the infant's casket, her mother gasped. Telling about the tragic loss of her friend Betsey and the ensuing recovery of her quilt brought back the turmoil of her joy at the cost of sorrow, and she had to stop and wipe her eyes before she could go on.

"Oh, my. Oh, my," her mother repeated over and over, shaking her head and blotting her damp cheeks.

Her father listened in silence until she related the details of Phillip's disappearance, her resulting bitterness, and Darby Carter's shocking discovery. Then his whispered, "Oh, my little girl," almost derailed her determination to tell the whole truth.

As she confessed her perfidious use of the money her parents had sent with her, they listened, white-faced. But when, her eyes on her hands squeezed tightly together in her lap, she halting choked out the account of Grace's birth and her heartless abandonment of their granddaughter, her mother's sharp cry pierced her heart like a dagger.

Lillian drew in a ragged breath then lifted her pale face and declared contritely, "I have confessed all my sins to God and He has forgiven me, but I need to ask you if you could find it in your heart to forgive me, too."

As Eleanor Cartwright slipped an arm around her daughter's shoulders, Austin Cartwright proclaimed the pardon Lillian desperately needed to hear.

"We will always love you, Lillian Louise, and you will always be our dear daughter. You are forgiven."

Their three-fold embrace afforded healing for each of them.

* * *

Lillian woke the next morning, surprised to hear the grandfather clock in the parlor striking ten o'clock. Leaping from her poster bed in her childhood bedroom, she crossed the floor to the armoire, hoping she'd find something from her youth to wear for today. Portia had offered to launder everything in her trunk, stating that after such a long journey her garments would no doubt need freshening.

When she opened the cedar-lined wardrobe, the familiar smell sent Lillian's emotions to her throat. The last time she'd opened these doors, it was to pack her trunk for the trip west. Swallowing hard, she reviewed the few items that her mother had not disposed of: three dresses that were girlish and out of date, a pair of button-up shoes with pointed toes, a frilly petticoat, and—she gasped—her wedding dress!

Seeing the dress she'd chosen with such joy and hope for the future sent a wave of pain sweeping over her that doubled her in half; she had to clutch the door to steady herself. But as she squeezed her eyes shut and stifled a groan, she suddenly realized that even if she could go back and change things, she wouldn't; despite the tragedy and sorrow, she would still choose to marry Phillip.

She sighed and straightened her shoulders, feeling a sense of relief as a new measure of peace and calm settled over her heart and mind.

Quickly making a selection, she dressed and headed down the stairs, surprised to find that she was humming under her breath—just as she had often done when she was a girl.

Lillian heard the murmur of soft voices in the dining room, and she reached the doorway in time to hear Nora say, "I've kept the coffee hot for Miss Lillian."

Eleanor Cartwright replied, "Thank you, Nora. I'm sure she'll want some when she wakes up."

Lillian stepped into the room, exclaiming, "Oh, Nora, you cannot possibly imagine how many mornings on the journey west I woke up and wished for a cup of your coffee. Mine never did taste like yours!"

"Sit down, Miss Lillian—I set up for you in your old place—and I'll bring you a cup. And some breakfast, too. You still like currant scones?" Nora chuckled. "I remember how you used to pick out the currants and save them until you'd eaten all the pastry." The three women laughed together like old times.

As Nora left the room, Lillian turned to her mother. "I'm so glad Nora is still with you. And her husband, Robert—is he still doing the gardening?"

* * *

Lillian leaned back in the copper tub and closed her eyes. How many times on the journey west had she dreamed of this very tub in this lovely room in her childhood home!

A rush of melancholy made her head pound as her mind transported her back to the desert; the beating sun, the merciless grit, the longing for a cool bath. She opened her eyes to dispel the memory, only to be confronted by the richly purple iris on its long green stem, as elegant as ever, in the stained glass window.

She sat up abruptly and climbed out of the tub. After Phillip disappeared, she had suppressed her memories, determined to live an emotionless existence. But now those memories seemed to haunt her everywhere she turned.

When she had toweled dry, she wrapped up in the dressing gown draped over the nearby chair and padded in her bare feet to the window. Peering through a section of clear glass, her gaze took in the garden below.

Reality faded. The garden was filled with guests. Phillip stood waiting under the ivy-covered pergola, eyes shining, grinning his crooked grin.

"Are you ready, my dear?"

Lillian gulped and turned. Those were the exact words her mother had said to her on her wedding day when it was time to join her father for their walk down the aisle to meet Phillip.

As Lillian's face crumpled, Eleanor Cartwright held out her arms. Lillian fell into them, weeping inconsolably. "Oh, Mama," she wailed between sobs, "why?" The sobs kept coming.

Eleanor rocked her daughter in her arms and let her cry out her pain, her anguish, her sorrow. And the comfort she offered was that which only a mother can give.

When Lillian had regained her composure, she returned to her bedroom, kept by her mother exactly as she had left it, to find Portia hanging her freshly cleaned and pressed garments in the wardrobe.

"Thank you, Portia. I never really appreciated you until I had to scrub my own clothes." She made a wry face. "And I burned my fingers a few times, too, until I got the trick of using the flatiron!"

"Ah, pshaw! You always were a little bit of sunshine, Miss Lillian." Portia's pale skin had blushed crimson at the compliment and she scurried out of the room.

Humming softly to herself, Lillian dressed and then sat on the cushioned stool in front of the round mirror over the dressing table. Grabbing up her brush, she ran it through her curly hair. As she stared at her face in the mirror, she mused that the eyes looking back at her were certainly older and wiser than those that had smiled at her day after day when she was a girl.

She shook her head; she must finish getting ready. She pulled her hair back and secured it with a velvet ribbon. This afternoon was the monthly meeting of her mother's missionary society friends, those dear women who had fashioned her wedding ring patterned "encouragement quilt" and embroidered it with the words that had spoken so poignantly to her heart in her darkest moments on the journey west.

She lifted her chin and drew in a deep, fortifying breath; there was no use delaying the inevitable.

She closed her bedroom door and slipped down the stairs. As she passed the kitchen, Nora stepped out, balancing a three-tiered tray of lemon tarts.

Lillian couldn't help the delighted exclamation that burst from her lips, "Lemon tarts, Nora? Would you believe I day-dreamed about your lemon tarts on my trip west?"

"Yes, Miss Lillian." Nora beamed. "Just for you."

Lillian leaned forward and dropped a kiss on Nora's round cheek. "You are so good to me!"

"You be careful now, Miss Lillian," Nora scolded affectionately. "You don't want to make me drop this!"

Lillian laughed and quickly stepped aside, motioning Nora toward the parlor with her tray of sweets.

Lillian hesitated in the hallway, momentarily overcome with trepidation when she heard the buzz of conversation coming from the parlor.

Then Eleanor Cartwright appeared in the doorway. "There you are, my dear. Come, everyone is anxious to see you."

Welcoming voices called to her.

"Is that you, dear Lillian?"

"She's really here, girls!"

And then she was in the parlor, surrounded by her mother's friends, being hugged and patted and kissed and complimented.

"Just look at you, Dearie. As lovely as ever."

"You are your mother's mirror. Isn't she, girls?"

"Here's an empty chair, come and sit by me."

When the fuss died down, her mother, ever the gracious hostess, welcomed everyone. "I'm so glad that it's my turn to host you all today. As you know, Lillian has been gone for almost seven years. And although I will admit that I hoped, I never allowed myself to expect to see her again, so today, my joy knows no bounds. While we enjoy the tea and tarts that Nora prepared in

Lillian's honor, you will hear an account of our dear girl's trip west, and in particular, the role her quilt and our prayers played in her adventures."

As all eyes fixed on Lillian, she again felt the weight of her grief and unworthiness. Then into her spirit came the words, the promise of Romans 8: *There is therefore now no condemnation to them which are in Christ Jesus, who walk not after the flesh but after the Spirit. For the law of the Spirit of life in Christ Jesus has made me free from the law of sin and death."*

Forgiveness has set me free, she reminded herself, lifting her chin. She looked around the room and drew in a fluttery breath. "I'm delighted to be with you today. When I learned that it was mother's turn to host your meeting, I could hardly wait to see you, to thank you for the quilt and for your prayers. I believe I am here today because of those prayers.

"The journey west was filled with hardship and heartache. Babies died. Friends died of accident and snake-bite. We were attacked by Indians. We barely escaped with our lives in a prairie fire. We crossed raging rivers, treacherous mountains, and a hot, dry desert."

She clasped one hand inside the other and squeezed hard for courage to go on.

"But when I lost my dear husband, my faith staggered, and I must admit that I lost my way for a time." Sorrow filled her eyes as she tried to be tactfully honest while avoiding unnecessary details. "Phillip and I have a daughter, Grace, who is six years old now. In my pain and despair, I was not able to care for Grace, so she is living with a friend."

Glancing around the room at the dear women who had faithfully upheld her in prayer, Lillian cleared her throat.

"There are no words to adequately express my gratitude for the quilt that was a constant reminder of your prayers offered in my behalf. Our merciful God has answered those prayers. He has forgiven me and restored me to peace in His presence."

She offered a small smile. "I no longer have the quilt; I gave it to Grace." She blinked hard to clear her vision. "But God is faithful, even when we are not. Grace sleeps every night with the quilt tucked under her chin—and I believe that your prayers have covered her as well as me."

Overcome with emotion, Lillian stopped, unable to continue.

Anna Brison, her mother's dearest friend, moved quickly to her side and voiced the question that shone on all their faces. "How can we best pray for you now, Lillian?"

Producing a semblance of a smile, Lillian answered on a shaky sigh. "My mother's heart longs to be reunited with Grace." She faltered then bravely continued, "And I do so want to discover God's purpose for my life, to be useful in His kingdom. That was my heart's desire as a young woman. That's why Phillip and I made the trip west. And even though he didn't get there, I still want to fulfill the dream God put in our hearts—the dream to make a difference, to bring the gospel to the lost, to see lives changed."

Her voice grew more earnest. "There are many broken, hurting people in the west. They have lost everything—possessions, significance, loved ones. And like me, they have resorted to wickedness and become bitter and heartless. So please, pray that God will use me to bring healing and redemption."

CHAPTER EIGHTEEN

Three weeks later.

Lillian stood on the porch of Phillip's parents' home in Boston, a brown paper package clutched against her chest. She'd written to them that first week after she arrived at her parents' home; she knew they deserved the details of their son's disappearance and death, something she had never given them. Oh, she'd sent a notice of his "death" after arriving in Sacramento, but bitterness had made her words short and terse. How could she tell them he'd run off with another woman?

She'd arrived late in the evening and spent a sleepless night in a nearby hotel. The prospect of confessing all her sins to Felix and Moira Denbeigh proved much more daunting than telling her own parents.

When Phillip's mother answered the door, Lillian found herself caught in an emotional whirlwind. She was immediately ushered into the parlor and seated on the stiffly upholstered sofa between Phillip's parents, who nearly smothered her in their obvious desire to be close—as if touching her was akin to touching their son. With a cup of black tea resting in a matching saucer on top of the package on her lap, Lillian began her story.

She rehearsed the details of the trek west, highlighting Phillip's passion for ministry, his fervent prayer over each situation, and even his skill at hunting small game.

"Sounds like Phil," his father commented with a short chuckle, "good at anything he put his hand to."

When Lillian described Phillip presiding over Elizabeth's and Betsey's funerals and officiating at Lewis and Sally Mae's wedding, his mother's lips quivered as she whispered, "He was always such a good boy."

"Yes, and he was good man," Lillian agreed. "He loved me," she continued, "even to the point of getting into a scuffle with a bachelor he felt had less than righteous intentions toward me."

Phillip's parents both laughed, proud and pleased to hear of their son's defense of his pretty wife.

Lillian stiffened her chin and breathed a silent prayer for courage to say what must be said. *God, please help me!*

"I want you both to know that Phillip was truly an honorable man. However, I am deeply ashamed that the same cannot be said of me." She took a quick, fortifying sip of her tea before meeting their puzzled gazes.

"I apologize for the brief note I sent you informing you of Phillip's death." She blinked away the mist that clouded her eyes. "You deserved better, but at the time, we didn't know what had happened to him."

"What do you mean?" Phillip's mother studied Lillian's face as if she thought she'd heard wrong.

Lillian hurried to explain. "I had just realized I was

pregnant, and we were both thrilled at the prospect of having a baby. But because I felt so very tired, I went to bed early one night while Phillip stayed up late sharing his faith with a woman from the wagon train. In the morning, I knew by the undisturbed bedding that Phillip had not come to bed. Then I learned that the woman he'd been speaking with was also missing. Along with two horses. The woman had a questionable reputation, so everyone believed Phillip had run away with her. I didn't want to believe it. But after a search party covered several miles on either side of our campsite and found no evidence of foul play, there seemed to be no other explanation. I felt betrayed, abandoned, and so alone. At first, I was upset at Phillip. But then I became angry at God. My heart turned hard and cold."

Wide-eyed, the two elderly Denbeighs stared at her. But when neither of them spoke, she realized they were shocked speechless.

Her voice wavered but she forced herself to continue. "A few months after we arrived in Sacramento, I gave birth to a baby girl." She shuddered and stared at her hands. "I-I was so bitter," her voice thinned to a frayed thread, "that I—I gave away our baby, baby Grace, your granddaughter." She shuddered again, "And with the money my parents sent with me, I opened a-a house of—questionable morality."

Hot tears of humiliation and shame swamped Lillian's eyes, overflowed, and trickled down her cheeks. Splashing into her tea and dribbling down her fingers, the drops formed damp splotches that spread on the brown paper package. She rubbed at them nervously with her fingertips—as if she could erase them—erase what she'd done.

Belatedly realizing Phillip's parents were waiting for the rest of her explanation, she stilled her hands and went on in a strained voice. "About three months ago I sold the business. I hired a stage coach and driver, and on the way we spent a night—at my deliberate request—camping at the precise site where Phillip disappeared. As we sat around the campfire, a wandering miner, a Mr. Carter, stumbled into camp. I was still so consumed with bitterness that when Mr. Carter referred to God, I started to stand up to leave. But then he pulled a leather-bound Bible out of his knapsack."

The silence in the room grew so thick that Lillian could hardly think. She pressed her lips together, gathered her waning courage, and lifted the teacup and saucer. After she passed them to Phillip's mother, who deposited them on the small side table next to her, Lillian clutched the brown paper package with her icy fingers.

"Mr. Carter said he'd found the Bible a-and a wedding ring on a—skeleton that had a—g-gash in the skull." She gulped. "Made by a-a tomahawk."

Phillip's mother clutched the arm of the sofa as she slumped against it. His father groaned and clutched his chest, and Lillian suddenly feared he was having a sinking spell.

But in the next moment, he rallied. "My dear girl,

we have believed, all this time, that Phillip is dead, so how it happened does not change the fact that he is gone." His sensible assessment infused Lillian with the courage she needed to continue.

"The Bible was inscribed with Phillip's name," she whispered. "It was the one you gave him when he graduated from seminary. And the ring was also Phillip's; it had our initials engraved inside."

Her breath hitched and then released. "So you see, Phillip did not betray his vows; he was an honorable man, full of character and integrity." She lifted the brown paper package and held it out to her mother-in-law. "And I know he would want you to have his Bible."

The grief-stricken woman took the package and held it, staring at it for a long, breathless moment before she gently removed the brown paper. Then her age-spotted hand reverently smoothed the brittle leather. Her lips twitched as she slowly lifted the cover and turned to the presentation page. With the tip of her index finger she caressingly traced the name of her oldest son, *Phillip Arthur Denbeigh*, written in her own hand with such pride.

Lillian felt the older woman's body quiver, but then she stiffened and in a surprise move, she closed the Bible and passed it back to Lillian. "Hold this for just a minute, my dear."

Pushing to her feet, Moira Denbeigh crossed the room to the oak writing desk that stood against the wall between the parlor's two tall windows. She raised the roll-top, picked up a bottle of ink, and unscrewed the lid. Selecting a quill pen from a cubby, she dipped it in the ink and then tapped it lightly to remove any excess.

As she returned to the sofa, cradling the pen to prevent drips, she said firmly, "Would you please open the Bible, Lillian, and find the family register; if I remember correctly, it follows the presentation page."

Lillian nodded and opened the Bible at the front, smoothing the pages until she came to the heading, FAMILY RECORD. She immediately saw that Phillip's name was listed below those of his parents and grandparents. And although the ink was faded, the entries were still readable.

Lillian glanced hesitantly at Phillip's mother.

The older woman smiled gently as she held out the pen to Lillian. "Please, my dear, write your name beside Phillip's," she whispered, steadying her quivering lips.

Lillian's fingers shook so badly that she stuttered an apologetic "I-I'll t-try." Pressing her wrist against the page to steady her hand, she wrote "Lillian Louise Cartwright" in the space titled *Wife's Maiden Name*.

Relieved to have made the entry without smearing the ink, she looked at her mother-in-law.

Nodding her approval, Moira Denbeigh pointed to the empty lines below Phillip's and Lillian's names. Her voice filled with tenderness, she prompted softly, "Now write Grace's name."

Lillian was forced to reach up and brush away the mist in her eyes in order to focus. As she wrote the little name, Grace, a fresh wave of forgiveness washed over her spirit.

"We want you to know, Lillian, that we love you. We forgive you, and we will pray that you will be reunited with Grace." Moira took the pen that dangled from Lillian's fingers, but she didn't stop there; glancing over at her husband, she smiled and added, "We have only one request."

Lillian found her voice and whispered meekly, "And w-what is that?"

"When you are reunited with Grace, you will please write to tell us so we can rejoice with you."

Their kindness was her undoing; Lillian buried her face in her hands and sobbed.

Phillip's parents, two dear saints, exchanged a glance of wordless communication over her head. Then they both reached out, placed their hands on her shoulders, and Phillip's father began to pray.

"Heavenly Father. Today we forthrightly proclaim mercy and forgiveness for our precious daughter Lillian. We know that You love her even more than we do, and that our forgiveness is only a reflection of the forgiveness You have bestowed upon us all. We thank You for revealing the truth about our dear son Phillip's death, and we forgive the ones who committed such an evil deed."

The elderly man cleared his throat. "And finally, we ask that You make a way where there is no way, that You bring about the reunion of Lillian and her daughter Grace. Restore the years the locusts have eaten. Give Lillian joy for her mourning and beauty for her ashes. Release from her the spirit of heaviness, and fill her heart with Your peace. It is with thanksgiving and gratitude that we present these, our requests, to You, and we will be careful to give you all praise and glory. In the mighty and precious name of our Lord Jesus, we pray. Amen."

CHAPTER NINETEEN

Six months later.

Lillian sniffed. Coffee. She stretched in bed and lay for a moment with her eyes closed. It was so still, so quiet; no swaying, no clickety-clacking of train wheels.

Then her eyes flew open as a surge of apprehension propelled her into sitting upright. Sacramento! She sighed heavily and sank back against her pillow, allowing yesterday evening's events to replay in her mind.

It was dusk when the train, wheels screeching and engine snorting, jerked to a stop in Sacramento. By the time she retrieved her trunks and hired a ride to the hotel halfway up Main Street, the sky was dark and a drizzle of rain was falling. Ignoring the whispers of several locals—they obviously knew her by sight and reputation—she checked into her hotel room.

Lillian squeezed her eyes closed on the memory; she'd hoped that being gone for a year and a half would be enough time for the stares and gossip to die down. But perhaps that was something she'd have to live with all her life. She shook her head to clear her mind and sat up, reaching for the silk wrap that matched her pale rose negligee.

Today was the day!

With a surge of excited trepidation, she swung her feet over the side of the bed and stood up.

Today marked the culmination of her repentance and restitution. The day she would meet with the ladies who had worked for her. The day she would go to the orphanage to see Barsina and hopefully discuss the best way to approach her daughter. And the day she would try to track down Jack Montgomery.

The cold chill that ran down her spine was followed by a flash of heat. *Oh, God, help!*

When Lillian had dressed and downed two cups of black coffee, she headed down the stairs, feeling relief that no one was in the lobby to notice her. She stepped out into the street, sniffing the rain-fresh air and squinting against the sunshine.

Instinctively, her glance veered to the left.

Everything looked the same—and yes, The Red Door was right where she'd left it. She swallowed hard and deliberately turned away, reminding herself that God had forgiven her past and that she must forgive herself.

She looked up the street, away from her shame.

And caught her breath in a little gasp.

On what had been an empty lot just past Ben's Mercantile, a new white church lifted a stately steeple heavenward, dominating the view. Immediately, Lillian started walking toward it, deciding that offering a prayer in the new church in this place of her disgrace would be an appropriate way to begin her first day back in Sacramento.

When the words on the church name sign, posted in the yard, came into view, she stopped and stared.

St. Matthew's Presbyterian Church!

How truly extraordinary. Could it be a divine sign?

Propelled by an inner sense of destiny, she crossed the street, climbed the steps, and boldly stepped inside.

In the vestibule, a small table stood against the wall to the left of the sanctuary doors. An open Bible and an offering box rested on its polished surface. Along the right wall, a wooden pew offered seating. Several copper plaques, displayed on the wall above the pew, drew Lillian's attention.

From a distance she read the title on the larger of the two: CHARTER MEMBERS. Curiosity immediately pulled her closer. She recognized several names of prominent civic leaders as she scanned the alphabetical list, but as her eyes moved down, Henry and Barsina Stowe's names appeared. She nodded; yes, the Stowes were no doubt pillars in the church. Her thoughts raced along an emotional pathway; perhaps her daughter Grace attended here with them.

Blinking back the prickles that suddenly stung her eyes, Lillian moved to stand in front of the next plaque, a much smaller one. DONORS headed the list of a dozen benefactors. Lillian perused the names, listed by last name first. Anderson, Paul; Axleman, Angus M.; Bevins, David P.; Barton, Neville.

Her gaze travelled slowly down the column.

Montgomery.

She stopped. Looked at the given name: Jackson A. Her eyes widened.

She looked again. Jackson A. Montgomery.

A tremor ran through her body from her head to her feet. No, it couldn't be the Jack Montgomery she knew; he was an avowed heathen. She shook her head as she dismissed the heart-stopping thought.

"Good morning. May I help you?"

Lillian swung around to see that the sanctuary door had opened while she was lost in memories. Framed in the doorway, a middle-aged man wearing a clerical collar smiled at her.

"Oh!" Lillian tried to hide her surprise. "Good morning . . ?" She lifted her brows inquiringly.

"Reverend Winston," the genial-faced man identified himself. "Sam Winston."

"Ah, yes," Lillian nodded, immediately recalling the name from Jack's reference to the preacher responsible for Henry's and Barsina's conversions. "Then you would know Barsina Stowe. I seem to recall she was a part of your congregation when you were meeting in the mercantile. I've been gone for over a year and it was dark and raining when I arrived last night, so I was surprised to see your new church building when I stepped outside of my hotel this morning."

Reverend Winston nodded. "We broke ground eight months ago and dedicated the completed building last week." He waved at the DONOR plaque, "We are so grateful to those who made it possible to be in a place of our own. I'd be glad to show you around."

Without waiting for Lillian's consent, the vicar invited, "Come this way." He turned back into the sanctuary.

As Lillian followed him, she voiced her thoughts. "The sign outside says St. Matthew's Presbyterian. That's the name of the church back East where I grew up and where my family still attends." She paused briefly then continued in a puzzled tone, "What made you choose that name?"

Reverend Winston stopped and turned toward her, his face breaking into a huge smile. He leaned over, reached between the closest pews, and drew a hymnal from the wooden rack on the pew back. Then he straightened up and held the book out to Lillian. "Thirty of these were donated, along with an equal number of Bibles." He chuckled and shook his head, "What else could we name our new church?"

Lillian took one look at the name engraved on the front of the worn hymnal and turned as white as the linen handkerchief tucked under her cuff. Her voice quavered, "Wh-where did you g-get these?"

"Like I said, they were donated. Anonymously."

Lillian grabbed the nearby pew to steady herself.

Reverend Winston frowned and eyed her with sudden concern. "Are you all right, Miss?"

Lillian spun around on her heel and fled out of the church, completely abandoning her plan to pray.

Reverend Winston followed her to the steps, calling after her as she hurried across the street, "God bless you, Miss."

CHAPTER TWENTY

Lillian pushed open the wrought iron gate and stared up at the spacious two-story Queen-Anne style house featuring rows of leaded windows, six chimneys, and two corner turrets. Her legs shook and nervous perspiration beaded her face.

At the bottom of the broad steps leading to the wrap-around porch with its beveled, oval-windowed front door, she stopped beside a lilac bush. A chill spiraled down her spine. Lilacs were not native to Sacramento—so how did one come to be growing here?

She shook her head; there was probably a reasonable explanation. But after seeing the hymnals in St. Matthew's church this morning, her imagination was too fanciful for her own good. She took a deep breath, squared her shoulders, and studied the sign over the door: HOPE ORPHANAGE.

Her breath came in spurts as she clutched the railing and mounted the steps. She hesitated again, then lifted her shaking hand and knocked.

While she waited for someone to respond, she fished her handkerchief from inside her cuff and patted her face. "Oh, God, help me," she whispered yet again; it seemed those four words had become her default prayer.

What if, in the end, there was no way to remedy her deepest wrongs? She had humbly confessed her grievous sins to both sets of parents, and their forgiveness had brought a measure of peace. But this was the last—and the hardest—of all the acts of repentance and restitution she'd felt compelled to carry out.

The final weeks spent in the East were filled with simple joys, yet at night, lying alone in her bed in her old room, the burden of unfinished business kept calling her to return to Sacramento.

With her heart overflowing, she'd kissed her parents good-bye forever—for a second time, and boarded the recently completed trans-continental railway train that would transport her all the way to Sacramento.

After her visit to St. Matthew's church this morning, she had contacted the "ladies" who'd worked for her at The Red Door, offering to set them up as independent, respectable women—and two of the four had agreed to take her up on her generosity.

But repenting to Jack.

And connecting with her daughter.

She was wholly at God's mercy in seeking their forgiveness.

She stood up straight and wet her dry lips with the tip of her tongue. As she took a bracing breath, the words of Phillip's father's prayer came back to her. *Beauty for ashes. Joy for mourning. Peace for her heavy heart.*

In the next moment the big door swung open wide. And a rich voice, thick and warm as blackstrap molasses, welcomed her. "De Lawd be praised!"

Plump arms wrapped her tightly in an overwhelming embrace that left her feet dangling several inches above the floor. She nearly fainted from lack of oxygen.

"Who is it, Mama Barsina?" A voice from the past, Jack Montgomery's lyrical Southern drawl startled Lillian back to her senses.

Barsina plopped Lillian down on her feet and moved out of the doorway, leaving Jack and Lillian staring face to face.

"Miss Lily Ann . . ." he breathed the words that were almost a question, "you have come back."

"Jack Montgomery." Lillian took a determined, purposeful step forward. "I . . ."

Jack didn't wait for an explanation; following Barsina's example, he folded her in his arms. He kicked the door shut and held her tight, rocking her as if he would never let her go.

Speaking of miracles . . .

Lillian's arms circled Jack's broad back and she rested her head against his chest, instantly disturbed by his familiar scent of leather and spice.

Finally, he bent his head and whispered near her ear, "Your eyes tell me something good has happened to you."

Fluctuating between heat and chill, she leaned back and lifted her face. "Yes, that's why I'm here," she acknowledged soberly.

He steadied her on her feet.

"Come." He drew her by the hand into the formal parlor to the right of the foyer. With a gesture indicating she should be seated on the horsehair sofa, he closed the parlor door, shutting them in, away from curious ears and prying eyes.

He took the chair beside the sofa and leaned toward her, never taking his eyes off her face. "Now, tell me all about it."

With bowed head she stared at her hands clasped so tightly together that her knuckles turned white. Then she nervously tugged on her handkerchief; she rolled it between her fingers, twisted it, and then wadded it in her fist.

Jack watched her, patiently waiting until she found her voice.

Her words were low and humble. "I came back because—" she lifted her head and met his intense gaze, "I learned the truth, Jack."

"The truth?" Again, he waited.

Haltingly, she told him about Darby Carter and the shocking contents of his knapsack. But as she related his tale about Phillip's skeleton with the tomahawk gash in the skull, the color drained from Jack's face.

He shifted in his chair and opened his mouth to speak, but she held up her hand to stop him. "No, let me finish or I may not make it through." She blotted her eyes with her balled-up bit of linen and drew in a jerky, shallow breath.

"First, forgive me for manipulating you into negotiating with Bert Jenks for that house. In my bitterness I turned my back on God and shut off my conscience." She nervously crossed and uncrossed her ankles. "I know now that I was already bitter before Phillip disappeared. You see, I thought that if I was good, then nothing bad would happen to me. But the trip west was so filled with heartache and tragedy that I lost my way. I kept trying to do better so God would be nice to me, not realizing that His love cannot be earned.

"The truth is, I might never understand why the deaths and tragedies happened. But I do know that experiencing them exposed what was in my heart. I discovered that I didn't really love God—or trust Him; at least not nearly so much as I was actually trying to gain His approval by my good works. And when bad things kept happening, I blamed Him. And concluded He must not love me."

She shook her head. "How very wrong I was! I've had a lot of time to think. And more recently, to pray. And I've come to understand that if we let them, our struggles make us sensitive to the needs of those around us—and they give us a platform to encourage others in difficult circumstances."

She continued earnestly, "When I was trying to find my way back to God, I read a couple of verses in Second Corinthians that made everything clear. *'Blessed be God, even the Father of our Lord Jesus Christ, the Father of mercies, and the God of all comfort; Who comforteth us in all our tribulation, that we may be able to comfort*

*them which are in any trouble, by the comfort
wherewith we ourselves are comforted of God.'"*

She gave voice to her thoughts on the redemptive purpose of her pain and sorrow. "When we've been hurt or disappointed we need comfort, and when we find that comfort in the Lord, we are to pass it on to others. I don't know how I got things so terribly mixed up, but I can see now, after also reading through First Peter, that we are not to be surprised when we go through hardships—and that our goal shouldn't be to escape suffering, but rather to identify with Christ by finding purpose in our trials and using them to further the gospel."

She smiled sadly. "Even though God has forgiven me, I still struggle with regret over my past choices, especially because of how I hurt others." She steadied her voice and met Jack's gaze directly. "I want to redeem the shame I've brought on God's name, so I've come back here to repent face-to-face and make things as right as possible."

With a faint glimmer of her old self, she made a wry face and referenced his repeated offers to purchase The Red Door. "You will be happy to know that I contacted my former employees, and two of them took my offer to set them up independently so they can live respectable lives from now on."

Jack nodded gravely but said nothing.

She leaned toward him and made her final confession. "And lastly, I abandoned Grace. I know God has forgiven me," silent tears slipped down her cheeks, "but I'm so deeply ashamed. I don't know if there's any room for restoration—or if it's even appropriate."

She swallowed her groan. No one had seen the depths of her depravity like Jack, and no one had greater reason to reproach her. Shame and sorrow weighed her down. Moisture dripped off her chin as she dropped her head.

Jack was instantly on his knees, grasping her hands. "I have news for you, too." He tugged lightly until she looked up. "Do you remember . . . when we first met, I told you I was a heathen—by choice?"

At Lillian's mute nod, he went on, "Did you pray for me—as you promised me you would?"

With drenched eyes fixed on his, Lillian nodded again and then scowled. "Phillip prayed for you more than I did," she confessed.

"Well, God answered those prayers." Jack's voice held triumph.

Lillian gasped and fell back on the sofa. "How—?" Her mouth sagged.

Jack released her hands and rocked back on his heels. "When you left, I was heartbroken—you surely know I've loved you since that first day when you so boldly corrected my pronunciation of your name." She read the truth of his confession in his eyes.

"As long as you were here, I had hope. But when you left, I fell into a deep despair. Barsina was very patient, but in the end she suggested I talk to Reverend Winston. And when I finally did, he confronted me with my sinful state and introduced me to Christ."

He squeezed her hands as he laid bare his soul.

"God has forgiven me for my sins, in particular for coveting what was not mine—you. He's filled my heart with peace and given me purpose."

Lillian straightened, then she eyed him curiously. "Jackson. Jackson A. Montgomery. Is that your full name?"

"Jackson Alexander Montgomery, that's me. Why?"

"I read your name this morning on the list of donors in St. Matthew's Presbyterian Church." Before he could speak, she continued, "And the anonymous donation of Bibles and hymnals . . . was that your doing?"

Jack cleared his throat. "Uh, let me explain . . ."

Her eyes narrowed. "Yes, I think you should explain, Jackson Alexander Montgomery!"

"I may have been a heathen, but when I saw you throwing out everything you believed in—everything that made you who you are, I asked Henry to stay behind to collect the Bibles and hymnals . . . and the lilac bush, too. He caught up with us before we stopped at noon that day; I hoped you wouldn't notice. I thought you might live to regret your decision . . ." his voice trailed off at the amazement filling her eyes.

When she didn't speak, he leaned toward her, again taking her small hands in his large ones. "I love you, Miss Lily Ann. I always have." He tipped his head and questioned earnestly, "Dare I hope you could love me back?"

"Oh, Jack—" Lillian's sigh was smothered as she leaned forward to kiss him.

At that precise moment, the parlor door opened. A girlish voice interrupted them, demanding, "Uncle Jack, why are you kissing my momma?"

Pulling back, Lillian opened her eyes to see her young daughter, a raven-haired image of herself, staring back at her over the now ragged wedding ring quilt that trailed from her arms. **GRACE**, embroidered in navy floss, filled the circle that met Lillian's gaze.

Sliding to her knees, Lillian opened her arms—and her heart—to both of them.

CHAPTER TWENTY-ONE

It was a bright, sunshiny day two weeks later when Reverend Sam Winston performed the ceremony uniting Lillian Louise Cartwright Denbeigh and Jackson Alexander Montgomery in Holy Matrimony. A table covered with the double wedding ring quilt that Barsina had skillfully mended and pressed stood at the far end of Hope Orphanage's back lawn. The word **LOVE** was displayed in the center front, Lillian's tribute to God's faithfulness to answer the petitions of her mother's friends who had made it for her and faithfully covered her in prayer. Two candles in silver holders, brought to California in one of Jack's wagons by Barsina, stood on either side of a Bible bearing the inscription, "St. Matthew's Presbyterian," and displayed on a silver bookstand.

Just before the service began, the Hope Orphanage children, all fifty-two of them dressed in their Sunday best, filed out of the house and took up their rehearsed positions along the wrought iron fence surrounding the backyard. Directed by Mama Barsina, the children sang the first verse of Charles Wesley's hymn in their bright, clear treble as Reverend Winston made his way across the lawn and stopped beside the table.

Jesus, lover of my soul,
Let me to thy bosom fly,
While the nearer waters roll,
While the tempest still is high.
Hide me, O my Savior, hide,
Till the storm of life is past;
Safe into the haven guide;
O receive my soul at last.

Pink rosebuds woven into an ivy wreath adorned Grace's curly dark hair. Wearing a pink silk dress and dispensing pink rosebuds along with their sweet aroma from a small white basket, the young girl giggled as she skipped on the slate tiles toward the table, to the accompaniment of the children singing verse two.

Other refuge have I none,
Hangs my helpless soul on thee;
Leave, ah! leave me not alone,
Still support and comfort me.
All my trust on thee is stayed,
All my help from thee I bring
Cover my defenseless head
With the shadow of thy wing.

Lillian tucked her hand in the crook of Jack's arm and together they followed Grace across the lawn. Although their pace was a bit more decorous, their faces glowed as they smiled and nodded at the friends who'd joined them to witness their joy.

Jack looked very handsome in a black vest and stiffly starched white shirt. His brown eyes twinkled, and his mop of unruly mahogany curls had been brushed into a semblance of order. And in his pocket rested a wedding band, a gold circlet engraved inside with "Forever Love."

Sheathed in a pale blue gown trimmed at the throat and wrists with white lace, Lillian smiled from beneath a smart, veil-fringed hat perched on her shining chestnut hair. She carried a handful of yellow-centered white daisies secured with a blue silk ribbon tied into an elegant bow. And a wide gold wedding band, engraved on the inside with two words, "God's Grace," was tied into the fine linen handkerchief tucked into her sleeve.

The children, their faces split in wide smiles, sang verse three with great exuberance as Grace, her basket now empty, led the bridal pair toward Pastor Winston.

> *Thou, O Christ, art all I want,*
> *More than all in thee I find;*
> *Raise the fallen, cheer the faint,*
> *Heal the sick, and lead the blind.*
> *Just and holy is thy name,*
> *I am all unrighteousness.*
> *False and full of sin I am;*
> *Thou art full of truth and grace.*

Jack and Lillian reached the table where Grace waited beside Pastor Winston. Swinging her basket, Grace skipped over to stand beside her mother.

Lillian smiled down on her daughter, her heart nearly bursting with joy as she reached out and caressed Grace's dark curls.

Looking up at Lillian with adoration in her eyes, Grace slipped her small hand into her mother's and whispered loudly, "I prayed for you to marry Uncle Jack and be my real mother."

While the guests chuckled in delight, Lillian met Jack's adoring gaze and blinked back her tears. *God, only You could bring about such miraculous healing and restoration in our broken lives.*

Mama Barsina led the children in singing the hymn's final verse.

Plenteous grace with thee is found,
Grace to cover all my sin.
 Let the healing streams abound,
Make and keep me pure within.
Thou of life the fountain art,
Freely let me take of thee;
Spring thou up within my heart;
Rise to all eternity.

And because the wedding guests knew Jack and Lillian's redemptive story, there was not a dry eye in the audience when Reverend Winston began the marriage ceremony with those intensely meaningful words, "Dearly beloved . . ."

Joyce Williams

AUTHOR'S NOTE

And so my little tale began and ended with a wedding, but the journey in between is based on my husband's great grandparents' trek west by wagon train. According to oral tradition, "Phillip," a young minister, and a woman from the train disappeared; Phillip's wife, "Lillian," lost her faith and opened a brothel. On her return journey west, "Darby Carter" showed up at the campsite on the precise date of Phillip's disappearance, producing the Bible, the wedding ring, and the report of the skull's tomahawk gash. In this case, to say that truth makes the strangest fiction is no exaggeration.

Except for the quilt's role, all the tragedies and struggles are adapted from the diaries and journals of real people who ventured west. Statistics indicate the overall deaths averaged at least one per family.

How often we mistakenly believe that "being good" will guarantee a pain-free life! Sin brought sickness, pain, and death into our world, and we live with the consequences. I hope *Quilt of Grace* has reminded you that no matter what your journey looks like, the Holy Spirit is with you—like Lillian's quilt—and His role is always redemptive. And if we trust God in those dark times, we will discover that He has not abandoned us; instead, He is always just a step or two ahead of us!

One of my favorite poems, offering perspective on suffering, was written in memory of a little girl named Janet. I share it with you:

A SPARROW FALLS
By G. Bradford*

THE QUESTION
From all the numberless flitting throng
Of sparrows, who would miss one song?
But God leaned down and whispered, "I care.
'Twas one of <u>My</u> sparrows, and <u>I was there</u>.   (Mt 10:29)

A little girl, all sunshine and laughter,
(And sometimes scoldings, with kisses after!)
And hurts to smooth over, and deeds to applaud—
A little girl fell! Where were You, God?
A little girl fell! God, why weren't You there?
Is it only for sparrows and such that You care?

If You're God at all—then You could have prevented
This nightmare of pain! So You must have consented.
I've always believed You were loving and good.
I'd like to believe <u>still</u>, if only I could.
But God, if You <u>love</u> me, how can You allow
Such unbearable pain as I'm feeling right now!

GOD'S REPLY
Beloved, I care! In the midst of your grief,   (Dan 9:23)
In the midst of your stricken and crumbling belief,   (Jer 31:3)
In the midst of the blackness of total despair,
In the midst of your questioning, Child—I AM there   (Heb 13:5)
"In the midst!" Not far off in some vague fifth dimension,
But <u>there</u>, WHERE YOU ARE, giving you My attention—   (Ps 40:17)

My constant attention—and not just today.
Since before you were born, I have loved you this way.
You're important to Me. Every hair on your head   (Lk 12:7)
I have numbered Myself! Can the tears that you shed   (Mt 10:30)
Go uncounted? Un-noticed? Nay, Child; here I stand
Close enough that each tear-drop falls into My hand.   (Ps 56:8)

224

Nor am I a Stranger to anguish—to loss.
My own Son was taken one day—by a cross.   (Mk 15:35)
I know what you suffer. I know what you'll gain   (Rom 8:18)
If you'll let Me walk <u>with</u> you into your pain.
I'll carry your grief, and your sorrow I'll bear.   (Isa 53:4)
You've only to reach out your hand—I am there.

Fear nothing for Janet. Your dear little girl   (Jn. 14:1-3)
Is safe in My house—and all Heaven's a-whirl
With the ring of her laughter, her quick eager smile,
And the things she's saving to show you—"after-while."
Yes, I could have prevented—but Child, you can't see
With My perfect wisdom. Trust Janet to Me.

Of course you will miss her, but while you are weeping,
Remember, it's only her body that's sleeping.
Her "self" is awake. Wide awake. As I said,
I am God of the *living*, not God of the dead.   (Mt. 22:32)
She trusted Me, and My sure Word comes to pass;   (Mt. 24:35)
"Who believes shall not die." That included your lass.   (Jn. 11:25)

Let Me walk with you now, through the long heavy days;
Let Me slowly begin changing heart-ache to praise.
Take hold of My hand, Child: take hold of My love.
I will lead you to joys that you yet know not of.
Your faith may be weak, and your trust incomplete,
But I'll not walk too fast for your stumbling feet.

    (Mt 12:20, Ps. 103:14)

*I have given credit to the author, G. Bradford, but have been unable to locate or contact him/her.